T0167286

THAT WRIGHT FAMILY!

A "NEIGHBORLY" LOOK AT THE FIRST FAMILY OF AVIATION

Ruth Lyons Brookshire

Order this book online at www.trafford.com
or email orders@trafford.com

Most Trafford titles are also available at major online book retailers.

Printed in the United States of America.

ISBN: 978-1-4669-0576-4 (sc)
ISBN: 978-1-4669-0577-1 (e)

Trafford rev. 12/21/2011

North America & International
toll-free: 1 888 232 4444 (USA & Canada)
phone: 250 383 6864 • fax: 812 355 4082

THAT WRIGHT FAMILY!

Bishop Milton Wright
Susan Koerner Wright
Reuchlin Wright
Lorin Wright
Wilbur Wright
Orville Wright
Katharine Wright Haskell

From Wilbur's birth in 1867 to Orville's death in 1948—a fictional-factual view of the Wright family.

Dedicated to my children

ABOUT THE BOOK

THAT WRIGHT FAMILY! is a combination of fictional characters who represent what people thought about the family beginning with Wilbur's birth near Millville, IN in 1867 to Orville's death in Dayton, OH in 1948.

Bowler hats, suits, vests and serious faces—the Brothers looked unapproachable, sometimes even sour. What were they really like? Did they ever laugh? How did they get along? Who else knows us besides our families? Our neighbors, of course? Do they share their opinions? Of course!

The Wilbur Wright Birthplace developed the character of Matilda McHenry, the fictional, feisty neighbor of the Wrights when they lived near Millville, Wilbur's birthplace. Matilda loved to express her opinion along with the latest "doin's of that preacher's family". Matilda and several other fictional neighbors promoted the Wilbur Wright Birthplace as re-enactors or with a Readers Theatre Group—THE NEIGHBORHOOD LADIES.

The LADIES script became the 2002 booklet, THOSE BOYS*!* This second edition includes more family dynamics and post-Kitty Hawk flight problems. In addition to the diverse attitudes about the family, aviation and the achievements of the famous Brothers, this account includes a listing of important events for each decade. The cover photo of the full-sized replica First Flyer is courtesy of the Wilbur Wright Birthplace.

I hope you enjoy this fictional-factual combination which examines the times and attitudes as well as the facts and situations which made the Wrights' dream of flight a reality.

Ruth Brookshire
2011

1860's

The American Civil War begins and ends.

Abraham Lincoln assassinated

Birth of Wilbur Wright

Birth of Mme. Curie

Formation of the Aeronautical Society of Great Britain

POPULAR SPORTS

Football

Cincinnati Red Stockings—Baseball

Roller skating

Manufacture of bicycles

BUSINESS AND DISCOVERIES

Union Stockyards built in Chicago by Octave Chanute

First carpet sweeper

Gold discovered in Wyoming

Diamonds in South Africa

MUSIC, ART, LITERATURE

Mark Twain, Charles Dickens, Louisa May Alcott

Sculptor Pierre Rodin

Brahms & Richard Wagner

MILLVILLE, INDIANA—1868

The major town of Liberty Township was a thriving community named Chicago, nestled in the rich farmland of east central Indiana midway between the small towns of Hagerstown and New Castle. However in 1854 the railroad company completely ignored this town, and constructed its rails near Mill Switch, a town a couple of miles to the west and one mile to the north.

A few years later, Milton and Susan Wright invested five hundred dollars of their wedding gift money to purchase a five acre rental property northeast of this newly renamed town of Millville with its 100 inhabitants, a general store, a doctor and two mills. Rumor had it that Susan Wright was already tired of packing and moving. Their oldest son Reuchlin had been born near Fairmont in Grant County, and their second Lorin in Fayette County. Susan was ready to plant her petunias and roses by the small frame house in 1865 where the third son, Wilbur, was born in 1867.

The New Castle newspaper reported the weather that week of April 16, 1867, as warm and balmy—"perfect for spring fever". No mention of Wilbur's birth, but very few births were announced at that time.

MATILDA MCHENRY replaces the newspapers. She always knows what's happening in the neighborhood. And, she's not the least bit shy about expressing her opinions especially about what the Wright family was like when Wilbur was a toddler.

Howdy there. Why don't you sit a spell here in the shade? I'm just helping the Wright boys with some chores around the place here. Miz Wright'll be right sorry she missed seeing you, but her and the preacher took that little one Wilbur and went over to Hartsville College. Well, now, I think that where she said. I ain't rightly sure where that be. My man Jake says Hartsville's over in Bartholomew County. That don't tell me nothing. Anyhow the preacher's probably gonna be teaching and preaching there.

Gonna be right sorry to see Miz Wright leave. This place has never looked so good. I don't see how she gets it all done with the preacher always gone. Of course Reuchlin and Lorin sure do keep the woodpile high and the water drawed. Miz Wright was a-hoping they could settle down here. You see them rose bushes over by the fence. She says they're gonna be yellow. Now it shore looks like she won't be around to see them bloom next spring. Just don't seem fair. But, she is shore enjoying them petunias she planted around the house. She done give me some of them seeds, and I'm gonna have me some blooms next summer.

But back to that there college they's going to. She says that's where she met the preacher. You didn't know she went to college? She shore does think girls oughta learn to read and write. Well, I reckon there ain't no reason she can't have a different idea than me. I don't hold it agin her. Ain't surprised you didn't know, getting her to say much is like pulling teeth.

But the preacher! Well, you know that man never stops talking. If he ain't a-talking, he's a-writing for one of them church papers, a-writing to his kin folk or a-working on his sermons. He's got these little brown ledgers, calls them his *Diary.* You ever hear the like a-that? Waste of good candles I calls it. I wonder if he ever writes how Miz Wright manages those three boys, a house, a garden, the milking, the chickens and the pigs with him being off preaching.

Course my Jake says Preacher Milton can cradle wheat with the best of them. Miz Wright says he was a farm boy afore he began a-teaching and a-preaching. He pert nigh keeps up with Jake when it comes to shucking corn. Would you believe we got 11 bushels to acres last year? But that Preacher Milton don't talk about crops. If'n you mention one of them secret societies or education, you might as well forget getting a word in edgeways. He ain't gonna stop until they ring the dinner bell, and I've heard him keep on after that. Jake says the man can talk the horns and tail off the devil.

T'ain't no wonder Miz Wright don't talk much. She ain't had no chance to practice. She shore can fix things though.

My Jake bought me one of them newfangled sewing machines a while back. Hannah and me was a gonna make ourselves new church dresses and shirts for the men folk. Oh, we had some good sized dreams. Well, you know new contraptions. You can't trust 'em as fer as you can throw 'em. The danged thing stopped. Couldn't move the wheel, the needle, nothin'. Miz Wright and the boys stopped by with some of that salve she made to ease my back miseries. I was complaining about wasting time and money when she asked if she could look at it. I figured maybe she was gonna try some salve—we'd done tried everthin' else. Well, she started a-fiddlin' with it, explaining to the boys what she was a-doin'. Opened it up, cut away a wad of thread, and the danged thing worked better than ever. She laughed when I tried to thank her. "You just sew some school dresses for Hannah and Carrie. That'll be my thanks."

Too bad that little Wilbur ain't so easy to care for as that sewin' machine. She's mighty worried about his big head. "He's top heavy, Miz McHenry. I'm fearful the wind will blow him over if I put a hat on him. What do you think?"

Her, a college woman, askin' my opinion! I was mighty pleased at that. "I ain't never heard of that kind a-thing." I tried to be a bit of comfort although I had to wonder. That little bugger had been a walkin' around since he was a bit more than ten months old. The preacher thought that meant he was real smart. I wanted to put a rope around him when he came into my house. He'd stand at the door of a room, look around for something to grab and skedaddle to get it. I was mighty happy Miz Wright took him with them to Hartville. I shore can't keep up with him.

How that family does move around! The preacher even went to Oregon afore they got married. Jake ain't sure where that is. Sometimes I wonder if Preacher Wright's gonna want to stay put up there behind the Pearly Gates. *Reckon the other choice wouldn't be too much to his liking.*

I know I shouldn't be talkin' bad about a preacher. But I am shore gonna miss Miz Wright and the young-uns. She's been a good neighbor. Pity is that she's not gonna see them roses she planted. I ain't never gonna know if the wind knocks little Wilbur over when he puts on a hat. Who's gonna fix my sewin' machine or bring me salve for my back? Who's gonna insist we send those gals of ours to school?

Well, I hope you get back by to see 'em afore they leave for Hartsville.

HANNAH McHENRY hurries through her chores these days, but she's not complaining. She has important goals, thanks to Susan Wright's insistence that girls need to attend school, even if it means working harder and putting up with all those boys who pull her pigtails.

Cassie and I are making pinafores. I still can't believe it. We're going to school! Ma finally changed her mind about girls not depending on their husbands to tell them all they needed to know. Even my older sisters didn't agree with her about that. I sure wish I could thank Miz Wright for teaching me my ABC's and pestering Ma about girls in school. Pa's real proud that I can already print my name.

Of course, we still have to do our chores, but that's no never mind. Miz Wright says we girls have the right to read, write and cipher. Why she even thinks I could be a teacher some day.

Know what I'm gonna do? Ma's got family down in the Carolinas when she was borned. When I learn how, I'm gonna write some letters and try to find them. I think that would make Ma real happy.

1870's

Chicago Fire

P. T. Barnum Circus

Custer's Last Stand

First US zoo in Philadelphia

Thomas Edison—phonograph

Alexander Graham Bell—telephone

World Exposition displaying the arm of Statue of Liberty

Carnegie introduced steel furnace

LITERATURE AND MUSIC

Charles Darwin—*Descent of Man*

Jules Verne

Hans Christian Anderson

Henry Wadsworth Longfellow

J. C. Harris—*Uncle Remus*

Gilbert and Sullivan

SPORTS

First Wimbledon tennis championship

First soccer match

First bicycle touring club

CEDAR RAPIDS—LATE 1870's

After only a year in Hartsville, Milton Wright was elected editor of the United Brethren in Christ newspaper published in Dayton, Ohio. They sold the Millville property and bought a house on the far side of the river in Dayton for $1800. Their twins were born there, but both died within a month. Orville Wright was born in 1871. Three years after that on Orville's birthday in August, Katharine, the only surviving daughter of the Wright family was born.

Wilbur settled into the Dayton schools where he was considered a quiet, serious student.

Orville was quite the opposite. He and a friend started off to first grade with good intentions. However, playing in the neighborhood barns turned out to be much more appealing than sitting quietly in a classroom.

Their father Milton continued to irritate church members with his constant opposition toward Masonic orders. The church leaders sent him and the family to Cedar Rapids, Iowa. As Bishop of the Mississippi Region, he traveled throughout the western area of the nation which kept him too busy to write his articles condemning those who disagreed with him.

Cedar Rapids was already a thriving town when the Wrights arrived. Business and manufacturing flourished. Coe College would soon be established. Reuchlin the eldest brother earned a teaching degree. The population of Bohemian descent farmed or worked in the related industries.

IDA SCHMIDT is confused about her new neighbors in Cedar Rapids. Sometimes she admired them. Other times she shook her head at the strange ways the five Wright children were allowed to grow up. She'll be happy to explain.

When I heard a preacher from Ohio was moving next door, I breathed a sigh of relief. Nobody warned me Bishop Milton had five children and spent most of his time traveling on church business. I have to admit Sister Susan keeps her house clean. I'm not sure how. Her back porch is full of rocks and bird nests, and Sister Susan takes a book with pictures of rocks, birds, animals and makes the children figure out what they brought in. Did you ever hear the like of that? Well, she says she and Bishop Milton think curiosity should be encouraged.

One time he sent them some sand from a beach along the Pacific Ocean. Sister Susan let me see it. I felt sorta strange you know. Got me wondering what an ocean would be like. I decided I'd be content staying here on the Cedar River where I can see the other side . . . but I still wonder about that ocean.

The older boys, they're finishing up high school. Reuchlin is going to teach school over at Adair. He's the quiet one, hard to get to know. Lorin's a talker, loves to tell stories. When their ma isn't watching, they tease Wilbur. He's the middle one—be ready for high school pretty soon. Why, just last month, the older ones put him up to smoking a grapevine cigar. When Sister Susan headed their way, they grabbed their fishing poles and ran for the river. Poor Wilbur got so nervous he dropped the cigar and the match into a sawdust pile. I reckon fires are one way of avoiding a lecture. We neighbors grabbed our water buckets and doused the flames before they did any damage. Sister Susan says Wilbur took that as a sign that smoking wasn't for him.

The other neighbors think those boys ought to spade up the back yard for a garden. At first I agreed with them, but I never did have neighbors who kept me so entertained, especially when they all chased that "bat" around. Now, before you get the wrong idea, I need to tell you Bishop Milton usually found something to bring the children when he had a chance to get home. That bat was a toy like nothing I ever saw. They said it was a heliocopter that some man in France made. When you wound string around what looked like a stem and let it go, the bat thing would go straight up in the air. Reuchlin and Lorin even got interested in this thingamajig and chased it around. That was a sight to see—all them young-uns laughing and running like kittens chasing a sparrow. Now if they had a garden, they couldn't have done that.

When they got tired of chasing, Wilbur and Orville wanted to find out what made the bat work. Orville wanted to make a larger one that would go higher and stay in the air longer. Sister Susan started drawing out the plans. That's the first thing she always did before she started to repair or build something. Never saw a woman do that kind of work. Her pa was a cabinet maker in Germany, and she used to watch him. Told me her family used to live in Virginny and came to Indiana by wagon when she was three. She'd stop and rest by the side of the road until they came back for her. "That's proof I wasn't born to travel much." She tried to joke, but I could tell she missed her pa and ma something fierce.

But I was talking about the bat, wasn't I? Wilbur and Orville gathered supplies and began following their ma's pattern. They worked hard, but the thingamajig didn't. They'd start scrapping over whose fault it was, but in a few minutes they'd walk off together arm in arm. I think it was Orville who finally took the thing apart to use as a pattern. They tried putting it back together, but it was too bent up from all the flights it had already made. Made me a little sad. I had enjoyed watching that family. So what if they didn't have a garden, and their pa sent sand in their letters and bought them bats? They'll have good times to remember.

So will I.

HANS WAGNER and his family were new arrivals from Germany. A very lonely, unhappy boy in Cedar Rapids, Hans was determined to attend school and learn English in spite of the teasing from his Iowa classmates.

When new boys move to my street, I think only they are two more to laugh at me. I believed not they be my friends. My family speak German, not the strange English I hear around me.

This boy Wilbur he always greet me. He very serious, very good student. Sometimes he say words I understand not.

One day teacher mark wrong his math problem. Next day, Wilbur come to school with other math books to prove he right. He not give up. That day I smile back.

He laugh not at my accent, not at my spelling or my wrong words. Instead he invite me to his house. I play army with his little brother. Then we run and chase this toy that go over my head before it fall. His mother invite to supper. I like not that Wilbur must wash dishes like girl, but I laugh when he tell stories to Orville and Katharine. I laugh more when he forget how story end and say "The boiler busted" before he start another story.

Later we look at books with pictures of birds and trees, even rocks. I learn much from them. Someday I buy many books for my house.

But always I stand straight now. I smile, and I work hard to say words right in this English. I remind myself I am as good as my classmates, even if I not spell all my words right. I learn.

Maybe I even make other friends like the Wright family.

1880'S

Benjamin Harrison, from Indiana, elected President
Queen Victoria of England celebrates Golden Jubilee
Bingo introduced
Electric lights on New York City streets
Jack the Ripper terrorizes London streets
Aeronautical Exhibition in Vienna

ART

Rodin, Renoir, Van Gogh and Cezanne

LITERATURE

Lew Wallace *Ben Hur*
Short stories of Guy de Maupassant
Nietzche *Thus Spake Zarathrusa*
Karl Marx
Playwrights Henrik Ibsen and George Bernard Shaw

MUSIC

Wagner. Tchaikovsky. Gilbert and Sullivan

SPORTS

American Baseball Association formed
Golf introduced in US
John L. Sullivan—boxing champion

RICHMOND, INDIANA—EARLY 1880'S

Milton felt called to Indiana to publish his own newspaper against the evils of secret societies. Susan was delighted to live near her family again. (Her parents, the Koerners, had moved from Liberty to Richmond, IN.) Milton now owned a farm near Adair, Iowa, as well as his farm in Grant County and the Hawthorn Street house which he had rented to another family while he was in Iowa. In Richmond they rented three separate houses rather than buying more property.

The home of Earlham College, Richmond, the largest town in east central Indiana, was situated on the famed National Road, making the town a cultural and population center. Reuchlin and Lorin began their college studies at Hartville. Wilbur and Orville continued school in Richmond where Wilbur joined the literary society. Sometimes he made kites for the neighbors or taught Orville and his friends to swim. But most of the time, Orville and Katharine were forced to find their own entertainment.

BETH PORTER, a life-long resident of Richmond, kept her sister informed about the new family who had moved in next door. Unlike the Wrights' former neighbors, Matilda and Ida,

Beth Porter did not approve of Susan Wright's methods of rearing children.

Dear Sister Abigail,

I take pen in hand after a busy season of canning and preserving. My cellar is full of those new glass cans of green beans, peas, tomatoes, peaches and applesauce. God has provided such abundance.

You asked about the new neighbors in your last letter. Well, I have to say we have been more blessed in the past. Fortunately it is a small family—only two boys at home and a little girl. I understand that there are two older brothers studying at some church college. I wondered what was wrong with Earlham where our husbands studied, but Mrs. Wright told me she met the Bishop at Hartsville College. He even taught there at one time before the church sent him to Iowa. I suppose it's a matter of where they feel comfortable, but I feel certain the education is superior here in Earlham.

I don't see too much the oldest boy here at home. That would be Wilbur, and he's a young gentleman in Richmond High School. After school he helps his father with the newspaper he publishes. I've been told that the Bishop's opinions about secret societies are so strict that a number of Brethren church members don't agree with him. The Bishop won't budge an inch on his opinions, and rumor has it that the church may split in two. Just between us, I suspect that's why he and his family have moved around so much. You can't say that family doesn't know about geography.

I do admire Wilbur, but that little brother Orville—always into something, taking gadgets apart and trying to put them back together again. He's always trying to make a penny on something. He and his sweet little sister collect bones for the fertilizer plant and metal for the junk yard. Makes his sister pull the wagon and do all the talking and asking. I don't know whether he has a timid streak like his mother, or if he's done so much mischief he's afraid to show his face. I do know the neighborhood dogs found that pile of bones and barked and fought the whole night through. They didn't make any pennies on that, but that didn't stop Orville. Little Katharine keeps tagging along wherever he goes.

Take the time Orville decided to save money by boiling up some tar and adding sugar to make his own chewing gum. Sometimes, I wonder if that Mrs. Wright is right in the head. *Letting him use her pans when anyone with sense would know his idea wouldn't work!* When I mentioned it, she just smiled and said Orville could learn from his mistake. Well, the whole street learned from that one.

Some say Orville forced Katharine to test that concoction. They say her teeth got stuck together and had to be pried apart with a chisel. Some people have a lot of imagination!

Let me give you the straight of it. Orville and his friends tried that tar and sugar. It turned their insides out. I'll tell you all the neighborhood lights were on that night. Next day their faces were nearly as white as my sheets. But not one word of reprimand from Orville's parents. If he'd been one of mine, we'd have visited the woodshed for quite a while—white face or sick stomach not withstanding.

And, there was the circus to pay for candy. Do you recollect that man named Miller who worked for the railroad? He went out West to hunt and brought back all those animals he shot. Paid to have them stuffed and put the smelly things in what he called his library. Somehow Orville found out about it, and somehow he and Katharine convinced Mr. Miller to lend them to him for a circus parade.

Orville hitched a pony to the cart which held the stuffed bear. The pony didn't much care for the bear smell so he tried to outrun it. Their parade ran right through my garden and Mrs. Gibson's petunias.

That didn't stop Orville. He and his friends planned another parade and some circus acts.

This time his friends would pull the carts. Wilbur even wrote an article for the big Richmond paper telling people about the parade and the circus performances the children planned. "Help a youngster earn some candy." I was surprised and embarrassed they printed it. Neighbors of mine begging for candy money! I packed up my embroidery and went to visit Mrs. Conklin three blocks over. No way was I going to watch such a demonstration on my street!

So many people lined the streets that Orville and the children lost their nerve about performing. Orville didn't get his candy money, and I, for one, thought it served him right.

The neighborhood got a little quieter when Orville took up woodcarving. I figured Orville probably used Mrs. Wright's knives for his carvings. He should have been helping me and Mrs. Gibson straighten up the damage he did with his parade, but he was "learning" to carve. For his birthday, Wilbur bought him a set of wood carving tools. They say Orville's good at it. I'll take their word for it as long as that house stays quiet.

But that was too much to hope for. Orville used his earnings from the metal and bone collections to buy one of them newfangled contraptions called a bicycle. It's not safe to go outside the house with Orville and his friends racing them things. What is this world coming to?

I heard yesterday at the emporium that the Bishop will be editing the Brethren newspaper in Dayton again. They plan to leave immediately. Wilbur won't even pick up his diploma from Richmond High School.

I do hope the next set of neighbors with be quieter.

ETHAN GIBSON is one of Orville's friends who flew kites and swam with him. He also helped with the parade and chewing gum. As far as he was concerned, Orville could always find some way to make life interesting.

Grandma made me replant the flowers the pony cart tore up, but it was worth it. Never saw that pony run so fast. What are we going to do without Orville? He talked his brother Wilbur into teaching us how to swim. They made the best kites in town. You know who showed them how?

Their ma. My ma sure couldn't do that. Ma bakes good pies and stuff like that, but she expects me to sit in the parlor with my hands folded. Orville's ma knows how to do lots of things, and she knows a lot of stories too. She says she reads for the fun of it. So do Wilbur and Orville. I can't imagine wasting time like that, not when Orville has one of his money-making schemes.

Wish I could move to Dayton with them. Richmond is sure going to be dull.

1890'S

Samuel Langley of the Smithsonian begins work in aerodynamics
First film shown in NY
Rubber gloves used in surgery
Gold strike in the Klondike
Nobel Prize established
William McKinley elected president
Gillette invents safety razor
The Spanish American War
First modern Olympics
Zipper developed (not popular until 1919)

LITERATURE

Sherlock Holmes—J. Conan Doyle
Alice in Wonderland—Lewis Carroll
War of the Worlds—H. G. Wells

SPORTS

Gentleman Jim Sullivan & Gene Tunney—boxing championships
American Bowling Congress formed
1st pro football game at Latroba, PA
1st American Golf Championship

DAYTON, OHIO

Dayton, the third largest Ohio city, bustled with industry and ideas. Its population consisted of hardy Germans and English immigrants, first generation Americans who moved from the farms to the cities and enough Irish to keep the town interesting. This was an era of imagination and invention, the backbone of industrialization. Man's imagination had no limits. While the economy had not fully recovered from the turmoil of the 70's, times were improving.

For the Wright family, the 1880's were a decade to forget. After they returned to 7 Hawthorn Street in Dayton, Wilbur took additional classes in Latin and played football. Many considered him the fastest runner in the high school he attended. He planned to attend Yale, but he was hurt playing a 19th century version of ice hockey. While the accident was not terribly serious, Wilbur did lose his front teeth, developed heart palpitations, and a severe depression. Instead of going to Yale, he became cook, housekeeper and his mother's caretaker. His mother Susan after frequent bouts with consumption passed away on July 4, 1889.

SUSAN, 1831-1889

Susan was the youngest daughter of the Koerner family in Hillsboro, Virginia. Her father, a cabinetmaker and sometimes wheelwright, had come from Saxony to avoid serving in the German army in 1818. The Koerners moved to a farm near Liberty, Indiana when she was a child. Young Susan learned about building and solving problems watching him work.

Her parents enrolled her at Hartsville College, also in Indiana. She studied literature and, more importantly, met Milton Wright. As a young minister, Milton planned a mission trip to Oregon and wanted Susan to accompany him as his wife. She promised to wait for him, but refused to go to Oregon. They were married a few days after his return. Being a shy person, Susan dreamed of a quiet, permanent home. That was not to be. Their three eldest sons, including Wilbur, were all born in different Indiana counties.

When they finally settled in Dayton, she gave birth to a set of twins who lived less than a month. Orville and Katharine were born on Hawthorn Street. While Milton's work had taken him over most of east central Indiana, she had managed a farm, their children, and the housework without complaint. She was devout, determined, resourceful and frugal; most of all, she believed in Milton's work.

After her death, Milton continued his work, aided by Wilbur, Orville, and Katharine. On her birthday and their anniversary, Milton visited her grave. He often took his grandchildren with him and told them about "the light of his life"—their grandmother.

Reuchlin had already moved West to avoid further problems over money between his parents and his in-laws. Lorin, after a brief stay in Kansas, returned to Dayton to start his own family. After his mother's death, Orville left school to open a print shop with his childhood friend Ed Sines. For a while Wilbur worked with them. After failing with two newspapers (one suggested by their friend Paul Laurence Dunbar, the Afro-American poet and Orville's classmate), they realized that odd-job printing would never support three young men.

When the bicycle craze hit Dayton, Orville and Wilbur turned from printing to repairing bicycles. They even developed their own designs—the Van Cleve and the Sinclair. But for Wilbur this was not enough. What could he do with his life? Orville was fascinated by the horseless carriage, but Wilbur joked that the new carriage needed to carry a sheet under it to catch all the parts which fell off as it moved along the uneven streets

.**JACOB HORNER**, a friend of Ed Sines, was glad his friend was free of his association with the Wrights in the print shop.

Well, I finally had a chance to talk to Ed today. He's a happy man to be working on his own. He assured me that he wasn't talking against the Wrights. He was glad they had success with their bicycle repair shop.

You gotta know Ed. He's one of those people who tell you more by what they don't say than what they actually put into words. Why, he's even thinking about courting that dark haired girl whose father owns the butcher shop. Seems like the butcher has a lot of odd-job printing he's hired Ed to do. He's been real good about telling the other merchants that Ed is dependable and prompt. Ed's picked up enough business to buy some new type.

Course he admits that he'll never be able to compete with the big newspapers downtown. They're able to put out a paper every day. Nobody can set the old type that fast, especially when you have to write the story yourself.

I asked him about Wilbur's health. Wilbur was a bit hard to get along with when the three of them worked together. Now that's putting it mildly. I was at the shop the first day Wilbur came into work. Now mind you, Orville and Ed had been printing together since they were in grammar school. Orville even built their first larger press out of a tombstone and other scrap parts. It was so good that one newspaper man told him he didn't understand how it worked, but it sure worked well. Well, here comes big brother Wilbur who folded papers for his father's newspaper in Richmond and begins telling them all they're doing wrong.

Orville just laughed and put him to work folding papers. If you know Wilbur at all, you know he sure didn't like that. He told them he wanted to write the stories and the advertising. Oh, yes, he wanted to be listed as Orville and Ed's equal on the masthead. Most people wouldn't have taken that too well, but Ed just began to whistle and check some copy.

How those two brothers could scrap! They argued over everything. Sometimes I think Orville started something just to get Wilbur going, but it was sad to watch. And worse to hear! What did Ed do? Well, he started smoking cigars. When they got too loud, he'd just step outside to smoke until they got tired of the argument and went back to work.

I did notice that Ed don't smoke no more.

TYPHOID FEVER

Another tragedy almost struck the Wright family. Orville contracted typhoid fever. Both the family and the doctor feared the worst. Katharine delayed her return to Oberlin College to help Wilbur care for him. It was while reading the newspaper to Orville that Wilbur found his challenge in life reading about the death of Otto Lilienthal, the engineer who flew gliders. Wilbur was reminded of Penaud heliocoptre toy they tried so hard to replicate lived in Iowa. He read everything printed about flight. (That didn't take very long.) He wrote to the Smithsonian Museum requesting material about aviation. He studied the birds. He remembered his childhood kites. Was it only the wind that kept them in the air? Could man fly? What would be the best design for a glider? Could it be controlled? How? The questions whirled around his head. He thought he might be able to make some contribution to these and other questions. He could hardly wait for Orville to recover so they could get to work on this new idea.

Orville's friends were concerned about his health although they were not above enjoying the temporary loss of their major biking competition. Jacob Horner was even more concerned about Wilbur's state of mind about his new idea.

RALPH O'MALLEY

Glad to hear that Orville Wright is recovering from the Fever. You'll maybe think I am a bad person, but I hope he stays weak for a bit longer. That will give the rest of us a chance to win a medal or two in the bike races.

JEREMIAH TURNER

Well, Orville should be back at the bicycle repair shop soon. He's the only one that understands my bicycle. Why, I haven't even been able to finish a race since he's been sick. Some little problem that none of the other repairmen notice—it's just plain annoying. But I feel sure that Orville will find the problem in two shakes of a sheep's tale and get it fixed so I can finish a race. He sure does enjoy tinkering.

Hope he doesn't get depressed like Wilbur when he got hit by the puck. I never did buy that story. I figure brother Wilbur just realized he wasn't as smart as he thought he was and used all that illness stuff to avoid failing at Yale.

JACOB HORNER

I stopped by to see Orville. He's laughing about Wilbur's latest idea—building a flying contraption. Just keep that under your hat, will you? I think Wilbur's mind is going. Flying? Men die testing those flimsy gliders. And they're engineers, and they understand building all sorts of gadgets. Now what does a bicycle mechanic know about that?

So what's Orville gonna do? Like always, he'll follow along to pester and tease Wilbur when he has a chance. Says if might even be fun!

DAYTON, 1899

The Brothers continued to live at home. Katharine returned to her Latin and Greek studies at Oberlin and ended her engagement to an Oberlin football player. The Bishop now concentrated on possible corruption in the church. A younger minister had been elected to replace Milton as head of publications. This was a position that Milton felt would be a good match for Wilbur's talents, and he watched the publication accounts carefully.

Wilbur was much more interested in his new challenge of aeronautics than a church position. His confidence had returned. After studying the material he requested from the Smithsonian Museum, he wrote to Octave Chanute, the Chicago engineer. Chanute had gathered information from Europe and with others intrigued by the possibility of flight. He and his protégés tested their own designs on the sands of the Indiana dunes outside Chicago.

Wilbur began by building his own over-sized kite in the back of the bicycle shop. If that went well, he planned to build his own glider. Orville was curious, but not overly enthusiastic about Wilbur's grand plan. Such intentions did not protect them from eligible women, or possibly worse, the families of eligible women.

RACHEL NESBITT is one of these women. A high school classmate of Katherine's, she had several ideas on improving Orville and Wilbur's lives as well as the life of her younger sister Trudy. With her head high and her back straight, she paced to and fro along the side of the vacant lot where the neighborhood boys usually played. Today the only occupants were the brothers from Hawthorn Street.

One more time. I am going to walk by them one more time. You would think that either Wilbur or Orville would glance this way. Oh, the things I put myself through for my baby sister. I just hope Mr. Nesbitt never finds out about this. But it's time for desperate measures. Nineteen years old already, and Trudy doesn't even have a beau calling on Sunday nights. Something has to be done to rescue her from being an old maid.

I can't believe that grown men would waste their afternoons flying kites. Don't they know that kite flying is for boys? Men teach their sons how to manage the kites and then go on about their business. Those two look absolutely silly—Orville out there running with a kite and Wilbur taking notes in that little notebook of his. Surely they could think of something better to do.

All I have to say is that if they keep up this kind of behavior, their bicycle business will fail exactly the same way their printing business did.

I wonder which brother would be better for Trudy. Orville is closer her age, but he's so timid. I remember Katharine telling me that he loved to play practical jokes. Trudy and I would have to do something about that. Mr. Nesbitt has no patience with such tomfoolery.

He tells me the Brothers make a deposit at the savings and loan every week. We women aren't supposed to understand such things, but I know repairing bikes isn't an occupation that lasts all year. Maybe they could start their own factory with their designs for new bicycles.

You know what else I heard? Over in Indiana they found gas on the Bishop's farm which makes thousands of dollars every year. Maybe it was hundreds. I was so excited for Trudy that maybe I misunderstood. Of course, there are four brothers and Katharine to inherit so Trudy can't expect to be rich. At her age, she should be thankful she has a sister who's finding her husband who is healthy, God fearing and works every day.

Well, finally they're heading this way. Would you look at those creases in Orville's trousers? You'd think he was on his way to church. Maybe Wilbur would be a better match. I know Aunt Gertie Fenster would disagree with that. It's a wonder the man isn't blind. When he was sick a few years back, he read the entire *Encyclopedia Britannica.* He does have some strange ideas. Aunt Gertie says the brothers climb out on their roof at night to watch the birds fly. The children tell me Wilbur is building some box thing with wings. Don't ask me why? I just know he needs a good woman to remind him of the important things in life—like responsibility to his wife and family.

Trudy has her work cut out for her, that's certain. Good that I'm here to help her. First, I'm going to invite them to our church social Saturday evening. Well, they're finally coming in this direction.

Oh, Mr. Wilbur, Mr. Orville, may I speak with you for a moment?

THE BOYS OF HAWTHORN STREET are not happy about losing their playground.

WILLIAM

Look at them old guys playing with that kite! That's the largest one I ever did see. How they'd git it into the air?

ANDREW

I wonder what that one is writing in that little ledger? Looks like numbers to me.

SAMUEL

Are they ciphering about a kite? I guess Ma and Pa are right. Those two are little off in the head.

WILLIAM:

We'd better skedaddle home afore those loony guys see us!

1900's

FIRST MANNED-POWERED FLIGHT by Wright Brothers
First zeppelin flight
Man crosses Irish Channel in balloon
Boxer Rebellion between Chinese and Europeans
Panama Canal now supervised by US
Martinique volcano destroys St. Pierre
San Francisco earthquake
JP Morgan stops run on banks
Theodore Roosevelt President
Fountain pens become popular
Methodist church established; Rotary Club founded
Mothers Day begun
Teddy bears introduced

MUSIC

Ragtime jazz popular
Caruso makes his first phonograph recording

LITERATURE & FILM

The Great Train Robbery First 12 min film—*Mutt and Jeff,* first daily comic strip
Peter Rabbit, Potter—*Anne of Green Gables,* Montgomery
O Henry short stories
Upton Sinclair's *The Jungle* leads to US Pure Food and Drugs Act

SPORTS

First Grand Prix motorcar race
Spitball ruled illegal
London Olympics—US won 15 of 28 games field and track
Ty Cobb begins baseball career
First Tour de France
National Ski Association formed
First American Bowling Club Tournament

HARVEY STEPHENS is a merchant friend of Octave Chanute, the Chicago engineer who has become interested in the possibility of flight. Harvey thinks that idea is pure poppycock

There are times I think my friend Octave has lost his mind over this flying craze. He has built bridges, designed the Chicago Stockyard and now he spends his spare time on the dunes of Lake Michigan testing his designs.

What surprises me even more is the number of people who watch him and his flying friends. I guess they like to laugh at the gliders—some with two wings, others with three or four smaller ones. Some designers attach the wings to their arms and flap them like birds.

Do these fools leave the ground? No, they crash into the sand. The pilots dig them out, repair them if possible and try again. The same thing happens. What a waste of time! What is the point? Of course, Octave enjoys advising all these young engineers. When he goes to France, he comes back with even more ideas, stories of men who stay in the air for a foot or more. Again I ask, what is the point? When I think of his ability to design and build . . . What a waste!

Right now he's helping a bicycle mechanic in Dayton who wrote for advice. I asked why he bothered with someone without engineering experience. He said this Wilbur Wright is a very logical man, plans everything, makes sketches, keeps careful records. Octave thinks he just might stumble into something that might help his flying friends. He even traveled to Dayton to meet this Wright fellow and was impressed by how well the glider was built. In the back of a bicycle shop, if you can imagine such a thing.

Octave suggested Wilbur test these gliders some place where the winds are steady, where people and trees are scarce. He also suggested landing on sand just in case the glider actually flew. This Wilbur and his brother took that advice, but they didn't listen when Octave suggested they needed a sponsor.

Octave explained that Samuel Langley is sponsored by the Smithsonian and can therefore focus his full attention on flying. Everyone expects him to be the first one to fly with a motor.

To my mind that makes Langley loonier than Octave.

But Wilbur and his brother insist they will pay their own way so they can stay in control. I don't see how bicycle repairmen could afford that expense. Let's face it. It's about time somebody locked them all up in a crazy house and threw away the key.

But on the other hand, wouldn't it be funny if those two mechanics found a way to fly?

KITTY HAWK 1900-1902

In the summer of 1900, Wilbur made arrangements to take his glider to Kitty Hawk, one of the sites recommended by the US Weather Bureau. Following Chanute's advice, Wilbur had written to the National Weather Bureau. Wilbur chose Kitty Hawk and wrote there for more information. His letter was answered by Bill Tate, one of the area's important people, who agreed Kitty Hawk would be perfect and offered his help in setting up their camp.

On the Outer Banks of North Carolina, the sands, winds, and privacy awaited the young men from Dayton. Only a few fishermen lived there. A Life-Saving Station was close by for assistance in a maritime disaster. Nags Head, a small settlement with general store, church and school was also within walking distance. However, the only way to reach Kitty Hawk was by boat. Many of the inhabitants of Elizabeth, North Carolina, didn't know anything about the remote area of what would be the birthplace of powered flight.

THE BOYS AT KITTY HAWK first laughed at the Brothers from Dayton who wore suits and hats every day and were building this strange contraption. However, they soon became fascinated by their new neighbors.

GIDEON

Would y'all believe they do their own cookin'? Mr. Orville makes the best biscuits I ever tasted. Now don't you go running to tell that to Ma! Mr. Wilbur cleans their tin plates and cups with sand.

IRA

That tent of theirs almost blows over in the night winds. They told Pa they was gonna build a proper shed if they come back next summer.

JEB

Y'all see them skeeter bites? They's covered with'em. Them skeeters bite through that netting to taste that there Northern blood.

IRA

Y'all think they'd give up and go home, but they don't.

GIDEON

Y'all oughta hear Mr. Orville play his mandolin. Told me and Pa he learned to play so he wouldn't hear all the racket of children practicing their pianos and horns along their street. Those houses must be real close to each other in Dayton.

JEB

I never seen men work so hard on nothing. My pa works hard on his fishing boat, but he sells the fish. Who would want to buy a big kite?

1901

GIDEON

They ain't buildin' no kites this year. This here's what they call a glider, and they got tracks on the Kill Devil Dune to help get it in the air. Mr. Wilbur stretches hisself out on it, and Mr. Orville holds the rope. When it hits the sand, they write how far they went in that little ledger.

IRA

Don't make no sense.

JEB

They's from up North. Y'all gotta remember that. And don't forget Tommy Tate's been on that flying thing, too.

GIDEON

Tommy made sure he was their favorite. He'd go by every day with a whopper of a fish tale. Some days last summer when the wind wuzn't blowing so much, they put Tommy on that kite thing. The Brothers held on to ropes at either end to keep it from going too high or coming down too fast. Watching Tommy holding for dear life, well, that's one time I'm glad I'm not the favorite.

IRA

I sure do miss them canned peaches Ma got from the general store when all the dried fruit is gone She told me the Brothers bought them all, plus some cans of soup. But this year they got their own eggs. Bought a couple of hens from Mrs. Tate and put 'em in a pen outside that shed where they live.

JEB

It's shore fun to watch Mr. Orville wavin' his rifle and whoopin' at them wild pigs who try real hard to get into their chicken pen.

GIDEON

Remember how they measured and wrote down everything in them ledgers. Well, they's doin' the same thing with this glider. They's tryin' to figure out something, and I sure hope our teacher don't get any ideas.

JEB

I sure ain't gonna waste my time with all that cipherin' when I'm growed.

GEORGE MONTGOMERY, Gideon's father, is one of the fishermen who enjoyed Sunday afternoons with the Wright Brothers. Other days when he wasn't fishing, he helped dig the glider out of the sand and push it up the track to the top of the dune so the Brothers could continue experiments.

Me and the life guards sure got a belly laugh the first time we seen them fellas from up North. Both a 'em dolled up in suits and vests and stoppin' every few steps to shake the sand outta their shoes. Sure ain't clothes fit fer Kitty Hawk. We done wasted no time askin' Bill Tate what wuz goin' on. Wuz we gonna have to load our rifles to protect our womenfolk and young-uns from the start of another War 'tween the States?

Bill explained, and I swear he done it with a straight face; they wuz a fixin' to fly. I thought old Newt Tatum wuz gonna fall offa the porch. We all knew man wuzn't gonna fly. Not unless them Brothers had wings under 'em Sunday hats they wore!

But the two a 'em got along real well with the boys. My boy Gideon insisted the Wrights wuz just downright interestin'. So we men took to walkin' by when they wuz a workin' to say our howdy do's and pass the time a day. My woman Emily wuz real curious about how they could eat without a woman to cook and clean up fer 'em. Sure put her nose outta joint when I told her how neat they wuz.

Course, they'd bought up most of the canned goods at the mercantile. I sure didn't miss 'em cans of soup. Emily could outdo any one of 'em flavors. Do sorta miss 'em canned peaches though. Good thing is them Brothers don't use tobaccy so we ain't got no real gripes.

When their friends from up North aint' here with their weird lookin' contraptions, we shoot the breeze with the Brothers on

Sunday afternoons. The Brothers tell some interestin' stories about lights that don't use kerosene, people talkin' into a box to people across town. We all reckoned they was pullin' our legs until the preacher's nephews went North and came back with the same tall tales about them new fangled inventions. Could be we is way behind the times!

And even if we don't cotton to this flyin' idea, it's fun watchin' the Brothers' friends tryin' to fly their contraptions. Some of 'em didn't make it down the track afore they fell apart. One of them did get off the dune for a few inches. We couldn't help puff out our chests 'cause none of 'em could stay in the air as long as our new neighbors. Not that we admit that's flyin', but the Wrights is doin' better than 'em other guys.

1902

But we wuz sure glad they come back this summer—after most of the skeeters died off. They shore do give us somethin' to jaw about. Y'all gotta admit there's just so many ways y'all can tell a fish story.

Bill Tate had been sayin' they might not be back no more. Mr. Wilbur wuzn't so sure they wuz ever gonna fly. That glider just crashed too many times to suit him. Mr. Orville told Bill that Mr. Wilbur thought they wuz somethin' wrong, and he don't know what.

I hope they figure it out, durned shame to work so hard and get nothin' outta it. Course, we all knew from the start they wuz a bit cracked in the head and headed for the loony bin. But the more we gotta know 'em, the more we wuz a hopin' we'd been wrong.

HARVEY STEPHENS isn't happy with the way the Wright Brothers are treating his friend Chanute after all he'd done for them.

Would you believe that the Wrights refused to test and rebuild Octave's gliders down at Kitty Hawk? After all he's done for them! He even arranged to have Wilbur speak about their efforts at the World Exposition in Chicago. Says the Wrights discovered that some of the formulae Lilienthal used to figure lift, whatever that is, were incorrect. You have to admire those Brothers. According to Octave, they build a wind tunnel out of an empty box and used a gasoline fan to provide the wind. Spent most of the winter testing the wings they'd been using. Wilbur convinced several of the aeronautical engineers in his audience that they ought to check out Lilienthal's computations.

Another thing that wounded Octave was their refusal to let him share some of their improvements with some of the other engineers he knew. I guess when they say they intended to stay in control of their project, that's exactly what they meant. Poor Octave, he doesn't know whether to be proud of them for what they've accomplished in such a short time compared to his own work or to be disappointed that they don't need him. He even wonders if they trust him.

Hate to say I told you so, but I warned him to forget that flying nonsense.

Octave called me today. He's headed for France. And what is one thing on his schedule?

He wants to tell his friends in England and Europe about the achievements of the Wright Brothers.

I figure it's easier to give advice than to take it. Too bad the Brothers weren't interested in working with electricity or motor cars. I could make us all a lot of money selling those.

MILTON WRIGHT—1902

Bishop Wright had very little to say in his Diary about Wilbur and Orville's new-found interest. Strangely enough his only comments during the first years of the Kitty Hawk tests were limited to a line or two in his diary about the boys getting some sunlight and fresh air down south. He did give them money for a telegram when they left for Kitty Hawk, but wrote about his granddaughter going to school.

In the late 1890's Milton was head of publications and also legal officer for the divided Church of the Brethren in Christ. The Bishops felt Milton's responsibilities were too heavy for one man so they elected a new publication's officer. Wilbur was Milton's choice as his replacement, but the Bishops chose Millard Keiter instead. As usual Milton didn't give up easily.

An audit, requested by Milton after rumors about misspent publications money, showed a potential loss of nearly seven thousand dollars. Milton alerted the church conference which dismissed Keiter, but Milton insisted on court action and humiliation. This time the Conference felt the church would not benefit from a public airing of Keiter's personal use of church funds.

Milton insisted that Wilbur join him in a letter writing campaign to the Bishops, explaining the situation and requesting support. The two court cases Milton brought against Keiter were dismissed, and Keiter requested an apology from Bishop Milton. This controversy and constant correspondence coincided with Wilbur's work on the motor and propellers for the Flyer. Wilbur managed to continue his own plans for a fall testing of a powered flight and also support his father's newest cause during the spring of 1903.

MABEL HASTINGS is the housekeeper for one of the Bishops of United Brethren Church in Christ. Most of the bishops have "visited" as they try to keep Milton from still another law suit or more questionable publicity for the church.

Here's another letter from that Bishop Wright. He was just here a few days ago, ranting on about the Keiter fellow. Of course, I wasn't supposed to hear that, but it was my day to dust the front part of the house, and that's where the Bishop has his library. I have to hand it to my Bishop though. He stayed calm while Bishop Wright was pacing back and forth raising the dust. I don't know what he's so all fired angry about. The Conference dismissed the other man, the Indiana courts dismissed the court cases—what does Bishop Wright expect them to do? Does he really think he deserves special laws so he can get his son a position?

Everybody ought to abide by the same laws, that's what I think. I'd say it, but nobody's gonna listen to my opinions.

Guess I'll put this letter on the pile with the rest of them. Had one from the son Wilbur last week. My, he forms those letters with care. It's a pleasure to see a good penmanship. I wonder if the Bishop is ever gonna open them.

Another bishop who dropped by says he was gonna save Bishop Wright's letters to start his fireplace this winter. The two of them laughed and wondered what old man Milton would say about that. I tell you, these Bishops are doing a lot of visiting these days. It don't look a bit good for Bishop Wright. Well, it serves him right for making such a fuss about it. The Bishops all decided to follow the Bible and avoid the courts. Like my ma always said, "Don't hang your dirty laundry on the line."

I heard once that Bishop Milton had another son and a daughter who lived with him in Dayton. I just wonder if we'll be getting any letters from them . . .

DOROTHY LUELLA KENDALL and Katharine lived in the same ladies' boarding house at Oberlin College in Ohio, one of the few co-educational institutions of its time. Like her father, Katharine always kept in touch with friends from her past. In 1902, she took time to visit her friend Dorothy.

My, it's good to see Kate again. But I could tell the last two years have been hectic. The good news is that the Bishop doesn't stop by her Latin classroom these days and spend the evening telling her how to teach. He's in some sort of church controversy and still travels a lot. Neither Wilbur nor Orville have married yet. To be honest, I don't think Kate's even looking for a husband.

I still think she should have married that Cunningham she was engaged to. I guess she took our little group of unengaged women seriously—The Order of the Empty Heart

But she gets enthusiastic talking about her brothers. Wilbur borrows her sewing machine to make wing covers. I had no idea what she's talking about. Seems the Brothers spend their summers or falls at some place called Kitty Hawk and fly gliders. I thought they were building bicycles. It's all too confusing for me, so I suggest we go shopping. Katharine loves hats.

But even at the milliner's she went on about Wilbur's dream of flying, how he was invited to speak in Chicago before a group of aero something or other engineers. When he started to leave, Kate took one more look at his clothes and called Orville to help. Orville loaned him a shirt and cuff links. Kate laughed at rescuing Wilbur from the rag bag. I still didn't know why Wilbur was making speeches in Chicago, but I guess he must know what's he's doing. She whispered something about adding propellers and a motor to that glider next summer. I hurried her out the shop before the other women started to listen. After all I did want Kate to help me with my shopping. I only have six months before my wedding and so many decisions to make. Gives me a headache just to think about it!

I was hoping we could surprise Kate and take her to a Dunbar poetry reading. He's quite the rage with his Negro dialect poems. He even read his work at the Chicago World's Fair. Well, I was the one who got surprised. Kate actually knows Paul Lawrence Dunbar. *He's been to their house. Her brothers printed a newspaper for him and gave him a bicycle before he was so famous.* I hear he works at the Library in Washington and doesn't make many public appearances.

Sometimes I wonder if Kate appreciates all she has—a cook-housekeeper, her own money from the teaching position, and a father with gas wells on his farm in Indiana.

And she calls a famous poet by his first name!

KITTY HAWK—1903

GIDEON MONTGOMERY, son of George and Emily, is one of the boys who hid behind a dune to watch the trial flights of the Wright Brothers in December, 2003.

I reckon the rest of the fellers got skeered off last week. That flyin' thing shore did make a racket. Jeb's dog took off like a shark was after him. Jeb says the dog hid under the porch the rest of the day. Most of the fellers ain't goin' be here. They said it's too windy to stay out here just o watch that flyin' machine crash again.

I see Mr. Orville tryin' to show John Daniels about that there camera-thing they brought along. They wanted proof the Flyer left the ground. Reckon our word ain't enough for them men from the North. But I shore wish I could trade places with Mister Daniels. Not that I expect that Flyer to get off the ground, y'all understand.

Well, I'll be goldurned. Mr. Orv done got that there thing into the air, sorta like a leaf bein' picked up by a breeze. All them men run over there, exceptin' Mr. Daniels. He looked at that bulb thing in one hand and scratched his head with the other. Mr. Wilbur, he starts measurin' and writin'. Both the Brothers start lookin' at the contraption. Looked fine to me, but they wuz a—testin' every bolt and shakin' their heads. Finally they motioned for the Lifesavers to help push the machine back up the dune. Shor wish I could get closer and hear what they's a-sayin', but I don't want Ma catchin' me. Well, Mr. Wilbur got into the air this time, went a tad further than Mr. Orville, but they still wuzn't satisfied. My hands wuz a-gettin' cold from the wind. I thought about leavin' but they wuz-a plannin' to try again. I figured a couple of more minutes wuzn't gonna hurt nothin'.

I thought the same way the next time Mr. Wilbur stretched out on that glider. And I'm sure as shootin' happy that I did. Mr. Wilbur went up, and he just kept a-stayin' up there. My eyeballs felt like they wuz frozen open. This time after they measured, the men started toward the airplane shed. Whatever it was they wuz a—tryin' to prove must a worked. They had stayed above the sand. I didn't dream it, did I?

Poor Mr. Daniels wuz helpin' 'em when a big gust of wind caught the flying machine. Mr. Orville, he jumped outa the way, but Mr. Daniels got tangled up in all the chains and what they called ribs. He wuzn't hurt none, exceptin' for a bruise or two. But he still didn't know if'n he took that picture.

Tell y'all a couple of things. I'm glad I saw it all. Mr. Daniels may notta got a picture, but I shore got me a memory. Tell y'all something else, I'm gonna stick to the boats and fishin'. No sense in doin' all that work and not getting' paid for it.

EMILY MONTGOMERY, George's wife, is one of those who watched the first powered flights. After years of doubting their dream, Emily became a believer.

You have to understand, I ain't got nothing' personal agin either Mr. Wright. Both of them have treated me with respect and courtesy. I didn't reckon men from the North could be that soft-spoken. But down here at Kitty Hawk, we believe God is good, the Devil is bad, Hell is hot, and God didn't intend for man to fly. At least we used to believe that.

Mr. Wilbur told George he chose this place because of the winds, the sands and the privacy. Believe it, we got plenty of all three. Kitty Hawk ain't nothing but sand. Well, there be a woods to one side where the Brothers hunt, but I shore don't know what those roots fasten to. The winds shift the sands around so much I have a different view from my windows every once in a while. Mr. Orville raves about our sunsets bein' so beautiful. I shore hope I get time to watch one of them some day. He raves about the skeeters, too but he shore don't think they're beautiful.

Addie Tate told me about the night Mr. Wilbur showed up at their house. Here was this seasick man dressed in a suit and hat like he was a-goin' to church. Wouldn't ya know it, Bill asked him to stay the night. Addie tried to signal Bill no, but Bill just went on and invited him to stay till he got his tent put up. Addie just didn't think their house and food would be good enough for a man dressed in a suit. Believe me, Addie Tate's got the finest house around these parts, and she don't let nothin' go to waste. Why, when the Brothers left their glider that first summer, Addie was over there with her scissors to get that white sateen they used on the wings. Made Sunday dresses for her little girls. Gave me some scraps for a new collar and cuffs for my Sunday dress. I do feel fine wearing that. You gotta say Addie ain't the least bit selfish.

She admires that Mr. Wilbur. He thanked her for letting him stay, for every meal she cooked. She says them Brothers was brought up right. They know about manners. Addie says the only thing Mr. Wilbur made a fuss about was the water. He wanted Addie to boil him a gallon every morning. Found out later his brother Orville had nigh died of typhoid fever so we reckon Mr. Wilbur had fair reason to be a bit leery.

We all reckoned they was a bit touched in the head with this idea of flying. That other man from Chicago and some of his friends came down a few times, wanting the Brothers to help them. The Brothers' flying contraptions was way better than theirs.

If us women tried somethin' like that, our men would lock us away. So we stopped peepin' out from behind our curtains and tended to our business. Too bad our men couldn't do the same! But every time that contraption came out of its shed, the men folk swarmed around like skeeters. Oh did they have stories to tell. Worse than them fish tales.

One of them told George that a man in Washington got fifty thousand dollars from the Smithsonian Museum to work on this flyin' craziness. Fifty thousand dollars? I can't imagine that much money. Why that's more than all the men in Kitty Hawk and Nags Head could earn in two or three years. And usin' it to play with them wings and wires! What is the world comin' to?

The Brothers paid their own way. Y'all gotta them credit for that. But they had their ups and downs, and I don't mean crashes. Back in ought one, Mr. Wilbur lost it for a while. I thought we'd seen the last of them. "Man is not going to fly, not in my lifetime." That's what he told the men helping them pack to go back to Dayton. He was pretty down in the mouth over their experiments with the gliders. They got into the air, but they didn't stay there long enough to please Mr. Wilbur. Why, the way the men moped around here all winter, well, y'all a thought it was their idea that failed.

But the Brothers came back the next summer. Whatever the problem was, they'd solved it. Made over a thousand glides. That man from Chicago said they broke every record, whatever that means. Mr. Orville even got real interested in flying.

Emily Montgomery continues her account 1903

This year, they came back with a motor and a propeller. Our men was besides themselves with excitement. They was already beginning to think about the stories they'd have for the winter.

Couple days ago, Mr. Wilbur stretches on that contraption. When that motor racket started, I stopped washin' my front window to watch. Mr. Orville ran alongside as Mr. Wilbur went down that rail they'd set up in the sand on Kill Devil Hill. Good thing I didn't blink, or I woulda missed it. Why would anyone wanta go that fast? Well, he went up in the air like a big bird. I just held my breath. Mr. Wilbur's such a good man, I didn't want nothin' to happen to him. My heart liked to stop.

I saw him pullin' and pushin' at the levers. That contraption came down as fast as it went up. I squeezed my eyes shut and gulped out a prayer. The motor stopped. Mr. Orville stopped yellin'. I knew something terrible had happened. Well, I ran to the kitchen for water and clean towels.

When I got back, the Brothers was both bent over somethin' that broke. Well, that's it! They finally got the message. Man ain't gonna fly. Oh, they can still probably glide a bit, maybe put together a circus act or somethin' like that. But Mr. Wilbur was all right, thank the good Lord.

As usual I was wrong about those Dayton boys. They didn't quit. They fixed what was wrong. On December 17, Mr. Orville set up the camera again and stretched out on that thing. I went to peel some taters for stew. Wasn't no way I'd watch that again. But I couldn't block out the racket of that motor.

I waited for the crash and the yelling, but it stayed quiet out there. I looked, but all I could see was the men from the Life-Guard Station pushin' that contraption back up Kill Devil Dune. Mr. Orville was at the camera. Wilbur was writin' measurements in his little brown book. My knees gave way on that one, and I grabbed the door to keep from fallin'. George waved and grinned.

Mr. Orville had flown!

But, I could see that they was plannin' to fly again. George explained later they hadn't stayed in the air long enough to prove that the motor powered the flight rather than the wind. Leave it to men to complicate life! I headed back to put the taters in the stew. It was up to us women to show some sense.

Mr. Wilbur insisted on trying again even with the wind gusting nothin' but cold air. Don't know where that boy of mine is. He'd like to have seed that flying machine in the air. I wrapped my shawl around my shoulders and settled on the porch with my knittin'. I wasn't goin' to miss this.

Mr. Wilbur got into the air with no problem. The motor didn't sound so loud. Could be I was gettin' used to it. But I sure didn't know what was holdin' that thing in the air. I wished I wasn't watchin'. I was so scared for Mr. Wilbur, but I couldn't turn away. I know I couldn't breathe. I sure didn't knit. I think I prayed, but I ain't sure. I knew I didn't want that motor to stop, and I sure didn't want to see that contraption fall. Finally, when I thought I couldn't stand it another second, Mr. Wilbur began to coast downward. Even I could tell that he was the one in control.

Over 800 feet they told me, stayed in the air for pert nigh a minute. *That proved the motor had powered their flights.*

None of it made no sense, but it shore had been purty. All of us rooted down here on the ground, and those two Brothers taking turns up in the sky. I feel like I was part of a miracle

The good Lord knows those Brothers had enough failures, but they never gave up. Makes me wonder if there's something I ought to try to do. Seeing something like that make you think.

Well, I don't have no time to try to figure that out now. George is gonna be mighty hungry. He only had a bite or two of grits this morning and nothing since. Come to think of it, I ain't neither. Think I'll stir up some pone to go with that stew and put some more wood in the stove to cook that stew faster.

DAYTON—1903

JAMES CLIFTON is a friend of Wright grandchildren who often visited the bicycle shop while the Brothers worked on their flying machine and sometimes joined them for evenings when the Brothers presented their puppet shows or Uncle Orville made candy. Like his friends, James was glad that the Wrights would be coming home from Kitty Hawk.

It's been dull at the bicycle shop. Charles Taylor, the mechanic, isn't half so much fun as the Uncles. Horace and Ivonette told me this morning that Uncle Orville sent a telegram saying they flew that machine they've working on in the shop. When I told Pa, he laughed and said they was pulling my leg. If the Uncles had flown, it'd a been on the front page of the newspaper. Pa was right. The paper didn't mention it.

I guess Horace is all happy because the Uncles'll be here for Christmas. Even their Aunt Katharine is smiling. Uncle Wilbur will be home in time to make the stuffing for the turkey. Their grandpa's been too busy clicking and clacking on that typewriter of his. Ivonette says he's sending articles about the flight to a whole lot of newspapers. But, like Pa says, Uncle Orville is up to one of his pranks, and he's got the whole family in on it.

I really don't care much about that. I just hope their Uncle Orville makes more of that caramel candy.

HUFFMAN PRAIRIE—1904

The Wright Brothers had won the race for air supremacy, but they needed modifications and more experiments before the First Flyer would be a practical aircraft ready for sale. Even though no one had ever flown, US and European governments as well as world industrialists had already set what they considered necessities for contract negotiations. The craft must carry a passenger or navigator, be able to fly in circles, reach and maintain an air speed of 40 mph, stay aloft for an hour, and be easily assembled and disassembled for transport by rail or truck.

The Brothers agreed they needed to stay close to their tools and shop. They decided to lease a 100-acre cow pasture eight miles outside of Dayton owned by banker Torrence Huffman.

It was accessible by two trolley lines, but otherwise private. A barbed wire fence and tree were two small challenges for take-offs and landings.

The Brothers also applied for patents. They had worked hard for their achievement, and they had no intention of sharing their secrets without recognition or compensation. Their Huffman Prairie priority was to perfect their craft before they offered it to the world.

All they needed to achieve that was focus, logic, and lots of hard work. They did not want reporters, cameras, or uninvited guests. Newspapers had not shown much interest in their Kill Devil Hill flights, and their distrust of the media was growing.

The Brothers chose to remain private and in charge.

RAYMOND POWELL lives on a farm adjoining the Huffman property. He's spent his spare time during the summers of 1904 and 1905 watching the Wright Brothers at their new camp in the dairy pasture of the Huffman farm. Despite their problems, Ray has faith in their efforts.

Yes, sir, I've been watching. But let me catch my breath. That Mr. Wright with the mustache, well, he durned near grabbed me today. For an old guy in his thirties, he sure can run a lot faster than I thought. I can't talk to you very long. I've got cows to milk, and Pa says cows don't like to wait.

Have I seen the Brothers fly? Not yet! I've watched them cut grass and build a shed for the flying machine. I've laughed myself silly watching them two chase cows out of the pasture. But let me tell you something, mister, them two are gonna fly. So, if you got any notion of laughing at their attempts, well, you just better leave now. I ain't gonna put up with people laughing. Lots of people have big ideas, but they don't do nothing about it. As I see it, nobody's got the right to laugh at someone who tries something new. I got faith in the Brothers.

Yes, I was here when the Wrights finally invited some friends and reporters out to watch their experiments. Let me tell you,

I took it personal. I durned near cried when those people left a—smirking and a-laughing because the Flyer didn't get into the air. I reckon the wind wasn't right, or maybe the motor was clogged. I don't know, but the Brothers'll figure it out. I still got faith in them. Besides, they did get off that rail for four or five inches, did that several times. I admit that Flyer looked like a lame rabbit trying to hop. I just wish I knew enough to help.

Heard them say something about the air being denser down South and, of course, they had sand hills to help launch the machine. Well, they just built themselves what they called a catapult, that's the thing over there that looks like an overgrown slingshot. I read where that Mr. Langley used a catapult when he tried to launch his craft over on the Potomac. His pilot spent a lot of time in the water. They shortened the tracks, and they worked on something else. I was too far away to hear what was going on.

In the spring they started building another craft. This was a bit longer and taller, and I heard 'em talking something about an elevator. Oh, how I wish I dared go over and talk to them. There's so much I want to know. But I don't dare.

Well, I told you so. In September, they took off, they stayed in the air, and they turned in a circle. A beekeeper by the name of Amos Root drove from Medina to see what was going on. That's nearly 200 miles from here. Mr. Root may be a beekeeper, but he sure is interested in new inventions. One of the other neighbors said that Root bought everything new that had a motor. I don't know about that, but the Wrights allowed him to stay around. He even wrote an article for his beekeeping magazine about watching the aircraft turn. I'm gonna find a copy of that magazine. It'll help me prove that I'm telling the truth about a flying machine.

But you know the best part was in October. I durned near missed it. One of the cows was calving, and I had to help Pa. But the Wrights were in the air. This time they had people watching, friends and some neighbors plus one or two newspaper men—without cameras. I could see the flying machine turning afore I got to my watching place. And this time, they kept right on going in circles. I counted fifteen or so before I got so dizzy I had to lay down and close my eyes. I was so proud, listening to those people cheer every time Mr. Wilbur turned that craft. I told you they could do it, didn't I?

Tell you something else. I'm gonna find a job where I can learn about motors. Pa won't be none too happy, but pretty soon I'm gonna milk my last cow. I'm gonna be a mechanic. That's where the future is. Maybe I can even learn enough to help build an airplane someday.

DAYTON 1905

For the Wright Brothers, experimentation was nearly over. They were ready to sell the airplane. Thanks to Chanute, the British and French were interested. Foreign officials and industrialists appeared at the Wright Bicycle Shop, but the Brothers refused to give demonstrations or allow any visitors to see the aircraft. Glenn Curtiss who would become their major competitor arrived, hoping to sell them a lightweight engine which he had developed working with his motorcycles. Curtiss asked a great many questions and impressed the Wrights with his understanding of the relationship between controlled flight and bicycles.

But the Wrights wanted contracts, not visitors. They contacted their local congressman about promoting their latest model craft for the use of the US Army. Illness prevented his actions on their behalf. Their letter joined those of other aspiring builder-aviators in the polite rejection pile. Feeling that the US was not interested, the Brothers began more serious, but very cautious, negotiations with foreign governments.

SADIE HAMPTON is one of several girls hired to help Carrie Grumbaugh, the long-time Wright housekeeper, when she needed help with the additional cooking and cleaning for these guests who often stayed overnight in the Wright home. As far as Sadie was concerned, she wished that the Wrights had never become famous and that sister Katharine had not appointed herself hostess and ruler of the household. She complains to her mother.

I don't care if positions are hard to find. I'm not going back to work for the Wrights. It was bad enough when it was just the two boys and their sister. The Bishop is away most of the time on church business, so I don't count him. But that Miss Katharine, I can't get along with her and her ways. "Sadie, polish the silver. Bake a batch of those tiny cookies. I'm sure some of the girls will be dropping by this afternoon."

Girls, my foot! A bunch of old maids, that's what I call them. Well, some of them are married. Miss Katharine is always going to some wedding or other or back to that Oberlin College where she graduated. That means washing and ironing her clothes, cleaning her hats. But the biggest problem is that she always comes back from a visit with a new notion.

Charlie Taylor who works over to the bicycle shop, he don't care much for her neither. The way she always goes on about his cigars. Just between you and me, I think he buys the stinkiest ones he can find just to irritate her. I would if I were a man.

It was bad enough then. But now we've got all those men coming here to see the Brothers about that there invention of theirs. Now you never know who's gonna be here for a meal. Of course, we were used to adding plates for Lorin's children.

They've practically lived over at that bicycle shop. The Brothers spoil them something fierce—playing with them, making candy, telling them stories using homemade tin puppets. Mr. Wilbur sent them some sand from Kitty Hawk, said the Bishop sent Pacific beach sand when they was just little tykes in Iowa. Those four young'uns, they're no angels. When they get rowdy, Miss Katharine or the Bishop put them in the closet, under one of the kitchen chairs or even on top of the icebox. You never know where you're gonna find them.

It's these other people we have to set a plate for at the last minute. Miss Katharine gets all sweet and syrupy with their requests. "Make sure you cook Monsieur's So and So's chicken with egg, no milk or flour.", "Do we still have some currant jelly for the biscuits.", or "See if you can find a recipe for key—sh". I don't waste any time on ones like that. Never heard of it, can't spell it, don't want to run to the mercantile for some strange ingredients nobody in Dayton ever heard of. I found out later they were asking for a quiche. The French have a strange way of spelling!

I wondered if they were even speaking English. Yes, I know I'm complaining. I should be proud to even know the Wright Brothers. Well, I guess they did do something special, but I ain't seen nobody in any big hurry to buy nothing.

The Bishop wasn't too keen on the boys wasting their time on that flying thing. He insisted Wilbur help him with that big hullabaloo among the Bishops that spring of '03 when the Brothers were working on propellers and motors. Bishop Wright never made too many demands on Orville. Never gave him a lot of credit either. Always gripped at Katharine. At first I felt sorry for her, but I got over that real quick.

Mr. Orville, he spends more time in front of a mirror than most women I know, presses his own trousers. None of us can do that to suit him. He thinks he can fix anything. Never gets dirty in that shop of theirs.

Now Mr. Wilbur, he don't care much about how he looks, or what he wears. That aggravates Miss Katharine no end. I wouldn't mind working for a man like Mr. Wilbur, but knowing my luck he'll probably end up with a wife like Miss Katharine.

KITTY HAWK—1908

The Wrights soon discovered that their negotiators had serious questions. Why didn't the US government buy the Wright efforts? Why hadn't the Wrights entered the numerous competitions for aspiring flyers? Why didn't the newspapers print more positive stories of their efforts? The negotiators simply didn't know what to believe.

The Brothers even traveled to Europe for further talks, but they still refused to demonstrate or show photos of the plane. Without proof, the interest remained moderate. They applied for more patents and filed court cases to protect their rights.

Meanwhile Glenn Curtiss had accepted the backing of the newly formed Aero Club with Alexander Graham Bell, and the later AEA, Aerial Experiment Association. Curtiss exhibited his aircraft efforts, winning both trophies and money. While the Wrights concentrated on sales and court cases, Curtiss experimented, flew, and captured the publicity the Wrights had shunned.

Now they had no choice. For the Wrights, it was time to show their achievements to the world and gain positive media coverage. They needed more space than Huffman Prairie. The answer was obvious. The Brothers headed for Kitty Hawk in 1908.

So did the reporters and the cameramen.

The media roamed the area and talked to the remaining lifesavers from 1903, the telegraph operator and the fishermen. To earn a headline, several reporters embellished previous stories of the Wright flights which annoyed the Wrights and some of the women.

EMILY MONTGOMERY who had seen and heard the 1903 flights was one of the irritated women.

Never thought I'd see them Wright brothers again. I figured they'd be rich and famous by now and too good to associate with common folk like us. They did their flyin', and now our men folk is doing the talkin'.

Mr. Wilbur and the lumber got here first with plans to repair their 1903 camp. Some folks around here had ripped off some of the siding to repair storm damage and had taken some of the stuff they'd left behind. Don't say much for us now, does it?

When Mr. Orville showed up with more lumber and all the boxes and crates, our men was plumb excited to see what the Wrights was gonna do next. My man George said they had to do some more testing. All them governments wants 'em to go higher and faster, stay in the air longer, and, would y'all believe this nonsense, carry a passenger. A passenger! What fool is going to want to ride that contraption? What's gonna keep y'all on 'em wings—ropes and chains? But our men hardly take time to eat a meal—especially with all 'em reporters with their cameras hangin'around.

They's even men here from New York City to watch these shenanigans. They's comin' out of the woodpiles, and fallin' all over each other to come up with some tall tale. One of 'em reported the Brothers flew ten or twenty miles back in 1903, that the life savers had their boats and safety stuff ready when the Wrights flew out over the water. Now, we women all know that didn't happen, but our men sure do enjoy makin' up 'em stories for 'em Northerners.

But, it's like I was tellin' Addie Tate, the Wrights is different this trip. Oh, they's still polite, but they's always in a hurry. I figure they's hopin' the reporters and the cameras won't keep up with them. Won't matter none, them reporters'll make up what they don't see.

The boys, they've noticed the difference, too. No singin', not much laughin' or talkin' down at the Wright camp. They're downright disappointed. Well, the Brothers finally took that Furnas who came with 'em on a flight. Looked like they was ready to prove to the rest of the country, maybe even the world, that they could fly.

But did the truth shut those reporters up? Maybe a little. But I got own plan to stop all this bragging and blabbing. I just told Mr. Montgomery there wouldn't be no grits and gravy on his breakfast plate if I saw one more mention of his name with one of 'em wild stories.

One other little thing more that boils my blood. Them reporters never asked a single woman what happened that day in 1903. You better believe we was all a watchin' from behind our curtains.

If all them tall tales is part of bein' famous, well, they can just count me out. I'd rather gather my eggs, cook my grits, and enjoy a sunset now and then.

LE MANS—1908

After much urging and overtures from the French government, Wilbur agreed to take the crates of plane parts to France. Katharine packed his clothes and hat boxes (Unfortunately she forget to put the hats inside.). Wilbur left for Europe leaving detailed instructions for the rest of the family. Orville would demonstrate the Flyer for the US Army at Fort Meyers and write an article for *Scientific American.* Wilbur even left him notes to follow. (Orville wrote it, but he didn't use Wilbur's notes.) This article is considered one of the best accounts of the Wrights' aeronautical efforts. Charlie Taylor, their part time mechanic, brother Lorin, and Katharine were to manage the Dayton bicycle operation.

The Bishop conceded that the flying thing was not just a dream and a hobby. He answered letters from newspapers and the curious public who wanted to know about the famous bicycle mechanics. He was also generous with paternal advice on handling fame, morals, and Wilbur's place in history. "Don't drink wine. Don't take chances. Remember what you have contributed to the world."

In France, Wilbur insisted on a demonstration area with sand and steady winds. This time he chose the small town of Pau near Le Mans in southern France. When he unpacked the crates, he discovered the airplane parts had been scattered during the customs search. He first suspected Orville of carelessness. Finding no English-speaking helpers, Wilbur was forced to do the assemblage by himself. Through all his problems and loneliness, Wilbur remained focused on the upcoming demonstrations. Crowds of people—royals, military, and the inhabitants of the region—flocked to Pau to watch this quiet man and the strange "Bird" which he planned to fly. Most of the French doubted that would happen, and they wanted to watch his failures. When he succeeded, Wilbur Wright became an instant celebrity.

In the small town of Pau, so many people bought caps like the ones he wore that the local stores ran out of stock. But Wilbur had only one plan in mind. Sell the plane.

MARIE BRIGITTE de PAU was one of the women intrigued by his serious, focused attitude and impressed by his love of his family and his humility.

Ah, vous are American, n'est-ce pas? Vous are friend of le monsieur Reet? We may not say his name well, but we here at Pau, we know who he is.

I admit, when monsieur Wilbur first arrive in France, nobody think he is able to fly. We French, we already fly—hot air balloons, gliders, the airship de Alberto Santos—Dumont. This Wilbur, we sure he just another big wind from Amerique. Bicycle mechaniques who fly with motor? Not possible! They say they have picture. Who sees it? We French, we shake our head and shrug. Non. Non. Non.

When monsieur Wilbur come to Le Mans, he, how you say, borrow a building. Then the crate and box come from Amerique, many of them. We wait for his workers, but monsieur Wilbur, he plan to hire men from here. Big mistake. He no speak French. They no speak English. He work more than they do. Many problem!

But he stay very polite, very humble. The enfant, they love him. He even take one boy for a ride in the air. Imagine! A boy from Le Mans goes through the air like the general and kings. I tell you something more. Le monsieur Wilbur is very timid with the women. His face, it turns rouge. I think you say red. But it turn whenever a young woman speak to him. Very different from the Frenchman!

He is very close to his family, very concerned about his brother who stay in Amerique. He write him letter every day. And every day le monsieur Wilbur receive many letters . . . from kings, general, very rich men, and, of course, from many women. But le monsieur, he always read first the letters from his famille. The other letters, they must wait. You think maybe such a man, he get the big head. But, for monsieur Wilbur, that is not so.

And his dog. Ah, the dog of monsieur Wilbur. This dog he have no home here in Pau. Nobody want him. We all yell go, go, if he come to us. Moi, I say it also. The dog is all skin and bone. His fleas, they eat more often than the dog. But the man who conquer the air, he wash this dog. He name him Flyer. Now, you not recognize this dog. He is almost handsome.

Le monsieur Wilbur, he is not like the other American who come to the south of France. Maybe it is because he is from Ohio.

This Ohio, it is a special place? People maybe treat each other better there? Or maybe it is le monsieur who is special? We watch him alone in the air above us, and it give us all hope. Maybe we should all dream more, work a little harder.

We French we know how to dream. Sometimes I think maybe le monsieur Wilbur is a little French. But, non, he no drink wine. He is timid with the women. He no speak French. Such a man cannot be French. French or American, ce n'est pas important. He make us all believe in the impossible.

That make him special, your monsieur Wilbur.

JEAN PIERRE is one of the local boys who is curious about the American and his plane.

I hear the noise of that flying machine when I go to the fields this morning. I look up and my brother Henri Claude wave at me. I rub my eye and look again. Henri Claude is in that flying machine. I yell, "Henri, if our father see you, you are in grand trouble."

I hear Father tell him to stay away from that crazy American. But Henri Claude not listen. He now go through the village to play with the dog, to watch the American clean and adjust his Flyer. He even teach le monsieur Wilbur a little French, and he learn a little English. What is so terrible?

But now, Henri Claude is on the flyer. Only kings and generals fly with monsieur Wilbur.

And my brother.

Henri Claude? Is he brave or is he fool. He wave, he shout a greeting to all of us on the ground. Father see him, shake his fist. Mother see Henri also. She smile. They so different, my parents. Father believe in work, work all the time, earn for family. Dreams are for crazy men. Mother, she believe that man must dream, that the French who dream are the envy of the world. That men follow dreamers, not workers.

I must hurry to the fields. I need to do the chores of Henri Claude, perhaps calm Father. But most I want to hear what it is like to look down on the world.

FORT MEYER—September, 1908

Although Wilbur had misgivings over the separation from Orville, he knew they must provide flying demonstrations on both sides of the Atlantic in order to sell the plane. As older brother and usual spokesperson, Wilbur naturally wrote detailed instructions not only about the Flyer, but also about managing the people around him.

Despite weather delays at Fort Meyer, Orville set new endurance records each day he flew. When he planned another demonstration of passenger flight, Thomas Selfridge, a student pilot and member of the group choosing US aircraft, insisted that he accompany Orville. Selfridge had spent a great deal of time investigating the plane and questioning every small detail. Knowing that the young pilot would pester him until he gave in, Orville conceded. The first three turns went well. Orville reported later that he heard a few taps which he had never heard before and a thump. Orville prepared to glide into a landing and investigate.

Instead the plane crashed. Spectators hurried to rescue both men from the wreckage and take them to the nearest hospital. Selfridge did not survive the operation for a fractured skull and became the first official fatality of manned-powered flight. Orville suffered a broken thigh, head wounds, several broken ribs and injuries to the back which bothered him for the rest of his life.

Katharine again delayed the start of her classes (this time as a teacher) to remain at his side for nearly seven weeks. With the help of Chanute and pilot and family friend Frank Lahm, she managed to protect the wreckage of the plane and arrange for an extension of the contract trials. In France, Wilbur felt certain that Orville's carelessness had caused the crash, and he should never have been left without supervision. It was Chanute who discovered the cause of the crash, a splintered propeller and calmed Wilbur's misgivings.

AT THE POST HOSPITAL

While some of the hospital staff tried to avoid Katharine's constant suggestions and questions about Orville's prognosis, nurse **ABIGAIL MORGAN** found a kindred soul. The Bishop, as usual, arrived to supervise his family's actions. **ABIGAIL MORGAN** is definitely on Katharine's side during the weeks Orville remained in the post hospital.

I'd like to bandage that man's mouth. I don't care if he is a church bishop. Raising a rumpus because Miss Katharine went to a hotel to get some much needed sleep! He insisted on telling all of us what to do, but I didn't see him sitting day and night beside Orville Wright reading to him or trying to keep him cheerful. You would think Bishop Milton Wright would give his daughter some credit.

That Miss Katharine! Some of the other nurses think she's far too bossy, but I say she has a lot on her mind. Her brother is hurt, the aeroplane or whatever they're calling it these days, is a pile of wood and wire. His passenger is dead. The Wrights might lose all chances to earn an army contract. Photographers and other aviation engineers sneak out to the shed where they stored the wreckage. Why can't they invent their own flying machines instead of trying to steal from the Wrights? It's enough to turn a saint into a sinner. Her other brother is flying in France, and he insists on long, detailed letters about both the crash and Orville.

Fortunately, Mr. Chanute and Mr. Lahm are here to help her control things. It was Mr. Lahm who made her go to a hotel to rest, and Mr. Chanute who identified the cause of the crash as a split propeller. You'll notice the Bishop did nothing to help the situation.

Miss Katharine and I had several talks about how women have to stay quiet and let the men take all the credit, even when the woman deserved it. She's not happy about her teaching position in Dayton. She says most school leaders don't want to waste time teaching women, and the women teachers were not permitted to teach the more difficult classes. Therefore, she's always scheduled for beginning Latin when she'd love to teach Greek.

I know how she feels. They keep me on the night shift so doctors don't have to listen to my observations about some of the patients. I am proud of those few women who have managed to become doctors. Wish I could be one of them . . .

Miss Katharine and I agree it's high time men realize that this is the 20th century, and we women will get the right of vote. This world will be a much better place when that happens.

1909

Life changed for the Wrights. Wilbur's careful choices of competitions led to several monetary prizes. Contracts to build the Wright airplane were negotiated with both European industrialists and governments. Orville planned a teaching trip to Germany. Both Brothers completed the trials at Fort Meyer and were awarded the contract they had waited for so long. In compliance with the contracts, they taught some young pilots at Huffman Field and others at what became Maxwell Air Force Base in Montgomery, Alabama. Together the Brothers opened their own factory in Dayton to supply the contracted planes for the US government. Orville supervised the training of new pilots and developed the ancestor of the airplane simulator to make the learning easier.

Patent trials and problems with foreign factories kept Wilbur busy in court and in negotiations. The Brothers seldom flew, but did allow their young student pilots to compete. During this period, competitive teams were rowdy and undisciplined showoffs. Members of the Wright teams were instructed to be in bed by ten and no drinking was permitted. They were paid between 25 and 50 dollars per day, depending on their time in flight, and never flew on Sundays.

One major exception to the team competition was Wilbur's decision to compete with Glenn Curtiss at the Hudson River festivities in New York City. For Wilbur, this would be his first flight over water (despite newspaper reports about ocean flights at Kitty Hawk). Wilbur and mechanic Charlie Taylor modified the plane to carry a rowboat in case of emergency.

After a few efforts in the winds of Staten Island, Curtiss decided against the competition. Possibly motivated by both the prize money and the opportunity to prove superiority over Curtiss, Wilbur took off from Staten Island, circled the Statue of Liberty, and flew to Grant's Tomb without mishap, leaving spectators in awe.

ERNESTINE VAN BUREN is a spectator for the flight only because the leader of her bridge club insists this flying machine had taken Europe by storm. Her friend insisted the Wrights were quite popular there, and their children should see this new invention. Ernestine saw no point in any of the nonsense, but she didn't want to anger her bridge friends. Her son Todd is of the opposite opinion.

Why in the world am I sitting here waiting to see a man-made bird? Oh, there's Emily two cars down from me. She has her two sons with her. And Annabelle Morgan' parked next to her. I think she likes to show off that she can drive as well as our chauffeurs. Now that they've seen me here with Todd, I'll have to stay.

No, Todd, you sit right here with me, under my parasol. This is all Annabelle's idea. She was in southern France last year, said everyone there was quite excited about this flying thing. She even had a chance to meet Katharine Wright, their sister. Says she's a charming lady and the French love her. But they're just such common people from a little town in Ohio. I just don't understand all the fuss. I'm perfectly happy traveling in our private rail car or in the back of this Rolls. Besides, Annabelle cancelled our afternoon bridge game.

Todd, stop that bouncing. Your father should be here instead of me. But, no, he and his associates are going to watch from the office windows so they won't lose too much time from work.

How much longer is this going to take? Todd, tell Trevor to uncork this lemonade. I could certainly use a sip or two.

Yes, Todd, I can hear the cheers. No, I can't see anything yet. No, I'm not going to lower the parasol. A lady must keep her skin pale. What is Annabella waving her arms for? Sometimes she is simply disgraceful. And Emilie is standing up, cheering. What is the matter with the two of them?

Trevor, where is my lemonade?

That box with wings in the sky? Is that what all this fuss is about? Todd, get back in the car this instant. Remember you are a Van Buren. Trevor, grab him.

TODD VAN BUREN definitely disagrees with his mother.

I'm going to see a plane fly. Thank goodness Mrs. Morgan convinced Mother to bring me over to the river. Mother had to cancel my dance instruction today.

Mama isn't happy about it. I don't think she or Father know anything except work, bridge, going out to dinner. Father doesn't even like baseball. Oh, I wish I had a brother. Or a mother like

Mrs. Morgan who likes to see new things. She even drives her own automobile.

What would I do without our chauffeur Trevor? I sneak out to the garage to talk to him every time I can get away from my tutors. Trevor told me that two brothers built this airplane, the motor and the propellers.

They did it themselves with the help on one mechanic. I can't imagine what it would be like to do something or my own without someone ordering me around or doing it for me. Trevor says when I'm tall enough to reach the pedals, he will teach me to drive. Says it's like being free.

There it is! Wilbur Wright is flying over us. Is that a rowboat underneath? Why? What keeps him in the air? I can see him, like one of my toy soldiers. Is that what we look like to him? Oh, one wing is lower than the other. What's happening, Trevor? Is he going to crash?

I can't cheer any more. My throat is dry. Oh, he's straightening up. He turned around Grant's tomb, and he's coming back. What does it feel like to be in the sky? Can he go through clouds? How far can he see?

Oh, Trevor, do you know? I have to find out.

I think flying must be freedom. Someday, I will find out for myself.

1910's

Wilbur Wright dies
Gandhi begins his passive resistance tactics in India
Titanic sinks
Haley's comet appears
Japan, US sign trade agreements
Pancho Villa invades New Mexico; army led by Pershing can't find him.
Panama Canal opened
Income tax begins
Prohibition begins
Women still struggle for right to vote.
First transcendental telephone call from New York to San Francisco
Air Mail route from New York to Washington DC
First air mail stamp issued
Albert Schweitzer opens hospital in Congo.
Labor uprisings in Massachusetts and London
22 million die worldwide in influenza epidemic.

World War I—1914-1919

Airships and zeppelins both used. RCF, later RAF, established. US enters war in 1917. Food rationed in both Britain and Germany.

Chinese Revolution establishes republic (outlaws pigtails)

Russian czar abdicates. Revolution follows.

DAILY LIFE, ETC

First permanent wave given by London hairdresser
Four women arrested for picketing the White House to protest the lack of Suffrage
Foxtrot and Cake Walk popular dances
Daylight Savings time introduced
Motorized taxis in major world cities
Oil drilling begins in Persia

INDIANAPOLIS, INDIANA—1910

The Wright Brothers realized that they could promote their planes better in Exhibitions rather than competitions where Curtiss and others excelled with lighter, more efficient aircraft. Time and energy which could have updated their first efforts had been filled with patent struggles, correcting substandard European productions, and slow moving bureaucratic government orders and payment. They convinced the owner and builder of the new Indianapolis Motor Speedway to host a week of flying events in order to promote their plane. Flights around the circular race track by the Wrights and their competitors would give spectators people a taste of what an airplane looked like close up and what it could do in the air. The Wright Exhibition team members would have the opportunity to try for records in altitude and endurance as would the other exhibiting teams in attendance.

Katharine, Milton, and Lorin would also be in attendance at the end of the week. Milton, of course, looked forward to reunions with his Indiana family and friends; he had a great deal to tell them. At the age of 81, he had flown over Huffman Field. His major regret was that Orville refused to go higher. That day in May was also the only time the Wright Brothers ever flew together. Wilbur was content to be the passenger while Orville did the flying. Orville had also piloted the flights for the nieces and nephews.

Unfortunately, despite a great deal of advertising and promotion, only a handful of aircraft teams attended. After watching both Brothers fly around the race track once, most people lost interest in flights although many potential pilots and mecahnics examined the planes on the ground. The flying highlight was young Walter Brookins of Dayton. One of Katherine's students, he had been fascinated by the work at Huffman Prairie. He learned to fly, and at Indianapolis he set a new altitude record of over 4,000 feet. Orville ran to meet him and Wilbur was not far behind to congratulate their young protégé. Those spectators close by reported the record holder's first word to his mentors, "That was cold. I thought I was going to freeze."

Exhibition attendance decreased as the week went on—partially due to rain. This was the one and only aircraft show at the Speedway, although balloons and fly-overs are still part of the festivities.

HANNAH MCHENRY DAWSON is the daughter of Matilda and Jacob McHenry of Millville. She and the rest of her family had been curious about the famous Wright Brothers. Could they have been the family who had once lived next door? Hannah only hoped she wouldn't stutter around such famous people. What in the world was she going to say? Mother Matilda would have pinched her earlobe and pushed her forward.

Why did I let them talk me into this? The interurban was filled this morning. When we arrived at the Speedway, the crowd had already formed. I never saw so many over dressed women in my life. I thought maybe we'd come to a fashion show instead of a flying exhibition.

It's situations like this that bring back memories of my mother. She would have turned to me with some loud comment like, "I'll bet she can't milk a cow and slop hogs in that outfit." Her head would raise and she'd march right past them. Now, I taught school for years just like Miz Wright said I had the sense to do, and I never mastered that walk. But, Miz Wright is why I'm here today.

Ma always talked kindly about that pastor's wife who lived neighbor to us outside of Millville. My son Jeremiah and I have been wondering if these Wrights could be that same family. I tried to tell Jeremiah that I couldn't bother famous people like that. They certainly wouldn't remember a neighbor girl. Why little Wilbur wasn't even two years old when they moved to some college where their father could teach.

Some folk said it was the same family, but I couldn't believe it. Jeremiah suggested that I try to talk to the father. I've heard that he became a bishop after he left Millville, caused all kind of debate which divided the United Brethren church, and then I heard he made a lot of money from the gas they found on his farm outside of Fairmont.

You hear a lot of things which may start out as truth, but get dipped in imagination before they get to you. Seems I recall two older brothers, but they were little when they lived on the farm. There's no way we'd recognize each other now; why it's been about forty years. I wish I could get a little closer to that aircraft. It does look like a bird in a way, but did you ever hear of a bird with a motor?

Jeremiah pushed me toward a small group of people surrounding an older man with white hair. I wasn't sure if that was the pastor. I certainly didn't want to make a fool of myself. Then I heard his voice and there was no doubt in my mind. That was Pastor Wright. Ma thought he talked way too much, and I remember he made the longest prayer over a harvest dinner I'd ever heard.

Of course, Ma didn't care much for him. Before I could collect my thoughts, Jeremiah had pulled me up to the front of the group. "My mother and I wonder if you ever lived on a farm near Millville."

The older man nodded. "My son Wilbur was born there. I remember it well." He pointed toward the man with the hat who was checking the aircraft. "Fine neighbors we had there." I looked from one man to the other. There was no doubt in my mind; the one he called Wilbur had a larger head. It was the largest head among any of the pilots. "Now, what would your name be?" he smiled at me, before I burst into laughter. Wilbur could find himself a hat. Mother kept mentioning that as she grew older.

I had to clear my throat before I answered. "My mother was Matilda McHenry. We both admired your wife so much," I added.

He clasped my hands. "The light went out of my life when Susan passed." He thought for a moment. "McHenry, seems I remember Susan speaking of her and her two daughters. She so hoped the two of them could attend school."

Imagine that, after all the people he had met, he still remembered my mother and his wife's wish for us to go to school. I moved away so he could talk to his other admirers. I wanted a good look at what that little boy with the big head had built.

I had to admit that Ma had been a little wrong. Pastor Wright was a pleasant man, not the uncaring husband Ma had criticized. I began to laugh. Ma had been half right about the wind blowing Wilbur and his hat away. It wasn't the wind that carried that boy into the clouds, it was the motor, wings, and propeller. I wanted to be able to tell Jeremiah's boys all about it.

You just never know where wonderful ideas are going to go when you add some old-fashioned hard work to them.

DAYTON—1912

Valiantly, Wilbur fought the patent battles in courts in both the United States and Europe. Although he won most of them, his own personal dreams of research slipped further and further away. Lorin and Orville managed Wright Aircraft, but Orville preferred teaching pilots in Huffman Field and in Alabama. Katharine and Orville worked with the architects on their new home. Wilbur's only recorded comment was that the wide upstairs hallway was a waste of space. They were immediately narrowed. The Brothers donated a stained glass window in honor of their parents to a church in New Castle, Indiana, where Milton had preached. It was to be dedicated in May of 1912, the day Wilbur died. Court cases and death interrupted his dreams of more experimentation.

GERTIE FENSTER, Rachel and Trudy's aunt enjoyed her afternoons on the porch of her house one block over from Hawthorn Street. She'd seen most of the visitors, foreign and American, who came to visit the Wright Brothers. She also remembered those days when she'd watched them flying kites or bird watching.

Oh, I know you're going to call me a nosy old woman, but I sensed there was something wrong with Wilbur that day in May. I was sitting on the porch crocheting a new set of doilies for Trudy's parlor when I saw Wilbur walking home from the railroad station. He'd stop to rest, and he looked around the neighborhood like he was seeing it for the first time. I thought then he was just tired from his stay in Boston and breathing in that soot from the train. I figured he stopped so often so he could breathe in some good Dayton air.

A couple of days later I returned Mattie Fogle's crochet pattern. We watched the doctor go in. He wasn't in there no time at all, and he surely didn't look worried when he came out. Mattie called me later to tell me Wilbur had a touch of fever and was just plain exhausted. All those foreign countries and strange cooking—that'd be enough to make anybody sick.

We all realized the illness was serious when Mattie saw the lawyer and Wilbur's secretary, that snooty Beck woman, go into the house with armloads of paper. They were inside for quite a spell. A couple of days later, the older brother arrived. I don't remember much about him. But he's been living out West for twenty, or was it thirty years?

I get a choking in my throat every time I think about poor Wilbur. You know the Brothers had bought land for a new house. They plan to call it Hawthorn Hill, maybe in honor of this little street where they lived a lot of their lives with their mama and the Bishop. It just don't seem right that a good man like Mr. Wilbur should leave us so soon.

But leave us he did, on May 30, 1912. Only 45 years old. Look at what he's done! Mattie's nephew works at the telegraph office. He says the family received more than a thousand telegrams. Mattie and me had a chance to go inside the Presbyterian Church where the services would be held. Never saw so many flowers in my life. We didn't recognize the names of half the embassies represented. We waited outside to see the procession to the cemetery. Strangest thing happened. Traffic stopped, the telephone switchboards shut down and the silence was so thick we could almost hear it. I know that sounds silly.

Then every church in Dayton began to ring its bell. In unison and in harmony, like someone had written the music for them. It was beautiful and sad and glorious all at the same time. Wilbur Wright was on his way home beside his parents.

Makes me ashamed to think I used to laugh at them two young men out there flying their kites. Who would have thought what they did with that idea?

MATTIE FOGLE is another neighbor who watched the Wrights in mourning.

I never saw anything like that Orville. He just wanders around. He's lost without Wilbur. He calls Katharine, and the two of them go on long trips in that car of his. I'm surprised he can concentrate on driving, the way he moves around. Don't know where they go, but he sure didn't look any better when he gets home. His brother Lorin and Miss Beck keep things running at the airplane factory. Orville just doesn't have any interest.

I'm sure Katharine feels that way too, the three of them being so close for so long without their mother and their father always traveling for the church. But she doesn't give in to grief. She makes it her mission to keep Orville eating and moving around. I know in my heart that without her, he would have died. He's a lucky man to have a sister like that.

1913-1917

It was no secret that Orville dedicated his time and efforts to maintaining the Wright Brothers' reputation as the first to make a manned-powered flight. Still timid with strangers, Orville avoided meeting with the New York Board of Directors at Wright Aviation whenever possible leaving such matters in the capable hands of his brother Lorin and Wilbur's former secretary Mabel Beck.

With Katharine as his companion, Orville sailed for Europe to fulfill their contract to instruct flyers. They arrived home to discover the Dayton flood of 1913. The original Flyer, photos (including the Daniels effort), and books had been stored in their bicycle shop and escaped major damage. Bishop Milton and a neighbor had to be rescued by canoe. Orville realized that a more secure place must be found for the First Flyer and other valuable papers.

He fretted about the increasing number of patent suits. Most of the suits were settled in favor of the Wrights, but now people were trying to collect money from them. People they thought were friends like Spratt and Herring who had visited them in Kitty Hawk, insisted the Wrights had used their ideas. Before his death Chanute had ceased to support the Brothers and assumed credit for mentoring the Brothers in technical aviation matters. Other inventors and aviators found reasons to sue them as well. Orville, inundated by worries, remained timid and aloof with strangers. Retreating to the comfort of his family, he concentrated on guarding both their privacy and the achievements.

THE SMITHSONIAN CONTROVERSY

Worst of all, the Smithsonian which was now under the direction of Charles W. Walcott, a friend of Langley's, insisted that the Aerodrome which crashed into the Potomac in 1903 was the first aircraft CAPABLE of flight. Glenn Curtiss took advantage of that idea and offered to help Walcott prove his theories. If the Wrights were not the first ones capable of flight, it might aid the Curtiss' legal defense in the Wright patent infringement suits against him.

In 1914 Curtiss set to work to rebuild and fly the Aerodrome. In 1910, the Brothers had offered the First Flyer to the Smithsonian, but it had been refused. The Smithsonian preferred the idea of the Wright's 1909 plane which was the first the US government had contracted. The 1909 plane became part of the Smithsonian exhibit in 1911.

Insulted by the continuing preference of the Langley efforts, Orville sent Lorin and a camera to the Curtiss restoration site where Lorn was recognized and his camera destroyed.

Orville's doubts proved true. Curtiss had made several changes in the wing system, mounted the plane on floats rather than Langley's catapult system, and, finally, after the first test, installed a Curtiss motor. Even then the Aerodrome did not fly for any distance. After media interpretation that the plane had flown, the changes were removed, and the restored Langley aircraft took its place in the main room of the Smithsonian. Orville was infuriated and insisted the First Flyer was not only CAPABLE but had been the first manned-powered flight. When Walcott refused to recognize the Wright achievement, Orville arranged to send the historic First Flyer to London where it would be appreciated. He did allow several exhibits before sending the plane to its new home in 1925.

That was not Orville's only plan for retaliation. He quietly began to buy stock in Wright Aviation until he had controlling interest. His first step was to dismiss the New York Board members whom he did not trust. His second step was to sell Wright Aviation for over a million dollars and rid himself of both presiding at meetings and appearing in court.

Orville was now free to continue his life-long love of seeing how gadgets worked and puttering around the house. He bought an island in Lake Huron where he concentrated on installing the plumbing, heating and electricity. He even designed and built the railway from the harbor up to the house. He modified his Pierce Arrow so it was more comfortable for his back. Not all of his puttering worked. When his secretary Mabel Beck bought an IBM typewriter, Orville took it apart. Unfortunately, he didn't succeed in his efforts to improve the design. In fact, he was unable to put it back together.

At the beginning of World War I, Orville was commissioned a major and sent back to Dayton as a consultant. These were the days when many groups honored the Wrights' accomplishments.

Orville and Katharine attended these but he seldom spoke. When he did, he was a strong advocate of airplane safety and increasing the number of airports.

From time to time, he would modify or experiment with aviation improvements, which included developing an auto-pilot device for the planes and initiated the slam-flip control which enabled a pilot to slow the plane down during a steep dive. The latter was not used until WWII. With a Kettering engineer, Orville worked on the Kettering Bug which was an auto-controlled rocket bomb. WWI ended before they perfected the idea.

In 1917, their father died and was buried next to his beloved Susan. Katharine and Orville remained at Hawthorn Hill where they gathered their grown-up nieces and nephews whenever possible. There, Orville enjoyed his practical jokes and a good debate with his new in-laws. Life was calm and peaceful, but that would soon change.

HAWTHORN HILL—1915

LUCINDA MARIE WILLIAMS is one of the Wrights' new neighbors after they settled into their new home which they called Hawthorn Hill. Originally delighted at the social potential of her famous neighbors, Lucinda soon became confused by their desire for privacy and lack of self promotion.

I felt so sorry for our neighbors—losing a son and brother just when they were beginning to enjoy being well-off and famous. I recollect that Mr. Williams and I nodded to Wilbur once when he stopped by the building site back in 1912, but we didn't stop to chat. Howard and I did plan a reception to introduce them when they moved in, but they were still obviously in mourning so we didn't intrude.

Of the three, Bishop Wright is the friendliest. You heard about his adventure during our Dayton flood, didn't you? He waited too long to leave their little house on Hawthorn Street, and they had to send a canoe after him. I guess he didn't want to leave that house where he'd raised his family. But this is a much more comfortable home. He does enjoy that front veranda with those pillars. Every day he carries out a stack of correspondence, and their butler follows with the typewriter for the table in front of the Bishop. If I'm outside inspecting my gardens, the Bishop always smiles and waves. One day he walked over to the fence to compliment my roses and petunias. "Those were my wife Susan's favorite blossoms," he confided.

His son Orville is just the opposite. That man loves to putter around that car of his. And how he loves to speed! I hear the Dayton police don't bother to write him a ticket; they concentrate on keeping traffic out of his way.

My husband used to worry at the way Orville neglected the aviation factory. It appears that their brother Lorin and some secretary who worked for Wilbur make most of the decisions. Howard would have given him some advice, but Mr. Orville just doesn't pay much attention to his neighbors. A great many famous people drop by to see him, but do the Wrights organize a reception to introduce any of us? It's as if he, his sister and his father are the only ones who exist. Quite frankly, this lack of courtesy annoys me.

But Katharine annoys me most of all. My younger daughter Bethany thinks she's wonderful because she marches for suffrage, has had a career, and traveled all over Europe with her brothers. Now she spends most of her time writing letters to her college friends. It doesn't bother Bethany that the woman never married or doesn't have any gentlemen callers. She even joins the Wrights on those suffrage marches. Yes, the Bishop and Orville march with Katharine. I don't know where such ideas come from, but I've given our chauffeur orders to follow Bethany whenever she leaves the house unescorted. I just hope I can trust him.

Another thing that irritates me about Katharine is that she's met all those important people in Europe, and all she ever says is that they are pleasant when you get to know them. My friends and I want to hear what they were wearing, how they talked, what they talked about. I understand that one of the women even went up in the plane. Katharine's done that, too, but does she talk about it? You'd think it was some deep dark secret. Either that or she doesn't think that we local ladies would understand.

After all she did graduate from Oberlin and is on the Board of Trustees. I'd be willing to wager she talks to them about her trips to Europe. Anyway, I don't bother to invite her to my afternoon teas.

You'll have to excuse me. I promised Howard I'd go through the newspapers and underline the quotes and important facts. He simply doesn't have time to do that kind of reading.

He's been worried about his investments in Europe with those Germans on the rampage. Says he doesn't know why the Wrights sold airplanes to them. Should have kept them for this country.

JACOB HORNER enjoys his mornings in the local barber shop. His friends always find some way to turn the conversation to their former neighbor Orville Wright. They don't see him often now that he's moved out of the Hawthorn Street area, but they have their memories and their pride in one of their own.

I know Orville took Wilbur's death pretty hard. He's always waited for Wilbur to come up with the ideas, but that's begun to change. He don't like them court cases and all them New Yorkers telling him how to run their aviation company.

Of course, we all know the Wright Brothers never did take advice too well unless it came from their Pa. Too bad Orville didn't send his Pa to argue them patent cases; never heard of a pastor who had so many law suits about this, that and the other. But the Old Bishop never cared too much about that flying hobby of theirs. Remember when we snickered about the boys going off to Kitty Hawk to practice flying? We knew they wouldn't be able to fly, even told to stay and work on their bicycles. At least, that was sure money.

But, we figured that going to Kitty Hawk was one way they could avoid the Bishop's nagging.

Well, that's all over now. I'm proud to say Orville pulled one over on them New Yorkers. Always did think he had a head for business. Remember how he and Ed started their own printing business while their classmates were still in high school? Did a good job, earned a lot of respect.

I hear he sold that factory for durned near a million and half for it, plus the new owners got stuck with the patent wars. He's right happy with his own laboratory where he goes to be by himself. Goes down to the aviation school in Alabama. Reckon with all that mess going on in Europe, they'll be needing some first rate pilots, and Orville will make sure of that.

Oh, and I hear he's going toe to toe with the Smithsonian Museum. They want to give that man Langley credit for the first aircraft. You know Orville's not going to stand for that.

Someone said he was thinking about sending their First Flyer to London to display it there.

Whichever way it goes, that science and political bunch over in Washington just don't realize they don't have a chance. Orville loves a good scrap!

MILTON WRIGHT—1828 to 1917

Milton was born near Rushville, Indiana. He worked with his brothers on the farm and later invested in Indiana and Iowa land. He also taught school and maintained his interest in educational matters throughout his life. He chose to marry Susan Koerner because of her devout spirit and humble manner—important characteristics for a pastor's wife. Unlike Milton, she did not enjoy travel and refused to accompany him on his mission trip to Oregon. During the train journey through the tropics years before the Canal was built, he contracted Panama Fever and only completed two years of his mission experience. A few days after his return to Indiana, he married Susan.

Like most men of his time, Milton was master of his family. He and Susan made sure their children could read, write and cipher before entering school. They included encyclopedia and other secular books in their library. When he traveled for the church, he wrote to the children telling them of interesting new places and situations. The children were also expected to write to him, and he insisted on proper grammar and clarity of thought. While he was strict with his own children, he enjoyed spending time with Lorin's children who lived in Dayton. Susan, and later

Katharine, despaired at his carelessness with coats and umbrellas which he often left on trains.

Although he was named a Bishop of the United Church of the Brethren in Christ, Milton's strong influences and convincing rhetoric ended in dividing the church between those who accepted secret societies and those who did not. Later in the 90's, when he argued against the newly chosen publication chief Keiter and wanted both legal and church punishment for his embezzlement, most of the other bishops felt the Church had had more than enough dissension. Realizing his lack of support, Milton retired as bishop in 1905 and devoted himself to his interests in genealogy, correspondence, his Diary, and the family.

During the months Wilbur spent in Europe in 1908, Milton continued to remind him of the evils of the world. At the same time, he reminded Wilbur of his importance to the world. One example was the admonition that while Orville and Katharine took balloon excursions, Milton suggested Wilbur stay on the ground. Milton was able to live comfortably on the proceeds of the gas well which had been found on his farm near Fairmont.

He visited Susan's grave at Woodland Cemetery and often took his grandchildren with him. Susan remained for him a shining example of a good wife. He often berated daughter Katharine for her independent nature and overspending. In 1917, he passed away quietly in his sleep and was buried next to Susan and Wilbur at Woodland Cemetery in Dayton after funeral services at Hawthorn Hill.

1920'S

League of Nations established; US Senate voted against

Warren G. Harding shot, Calvin Coolidge and Herbert Hoover win their elections

J. Edgar Hoover, director of FBI

Ku Klux Klan reborn. 18th and 19th Amendments for Prohibition and Women's Right to Vote. St. Valentine's Day Massacre, Chicago. Black Friday, NY Stock Exchange collapses

USSR formed, Trotsky exiled and later shot

Hitler establishes Storm Troopers, is imprisoned, writes *Mein Kemp*

Mussolini forms Fascist government, marches on Rome

Gandhi jailed for civil disobedience In India. Chiang Kai Shek, president of China

Air mail established, aerial crop dusting begun, First Space Flight Exhibit (Moscow)

Charles Lindbergh, Amelia Earhart and German Hugo Eckener cross Atlantic, Amundsen, Noble and Noole fly over North Pole, Byrd flies over South Pole. Graf Zeppelin flies around the world, first plane refueled in air, James Doolittle makes first instrument only flight. Aeroflot (largest world airline—USSR)

LITERATURE

Agatha Christie, F. Scott Fitzgerald, Sinclair Lewis, Eugene O'Neill, John Dos Passos, Ernest Hemingway, John Steinbeck, Booth Tarkington, Edna St. Vincent Millay. e. e. cummings, Robert Frost, T.S. Eliot, Wm Faulkner, Ezra Pound, Edward Arlington Robinson, Thornton Wilder, Vachel Lindsay

FILM, ART & MUSIC

Mary Pickford, Cecil B DeMille *The Ten Commandments, Mickey Mouse,* Douglas Fairbanks *Thief of Bagdad*, Will Rogers-radio and stage. Paul Klee, Charlie Chaplin, D. W. Griffith, Grant Wood. Museum of Modern Art opens. Jerome Kern, Louis Armstrong, Paul Whitman Band Tour, Irving Berlin, George Gershwin, Victor Herbert, Aaron Copeland first Guggenheim Fellowship, Toscanini conductor of NY Philharmonic, Charleston, slow fox trot

SCIENCE

Cushing brain surgery, Insulin used in diabetes treatment, Mesozoic dinosaur skeletons found in Gobi Desert, theory of auto-giro, insecticides first used, Kodak 16mm color film. Iron lung. Fleming and penicillin

SPORTS, ETC.

Babe Ruth sold to Yankees. American Football League forms, First baseball game and World Series broadcast. Harlem Globetrotters begin. Jack Dempsey Boxing champion, First Winter Olympics. Man-o-War retires. Knute Rockne and Notre Dame undefeated, Unknown Soldier buried at Arlington Cemetery, Emily Post—etiquette, First Birth Control Clinic opens, George Washington Bridge and Holland Tunnel open in New York, Ford assembly line makes 15 millionth car.

LAMBERT ISLAND

When Orville, Katharine, and Orville rented a Canadian Island for their one and only vacation together, Orville discovered the privacy of island existence. He bought a rocky twenty acres with seven buildings in Lake Huron and began making changes—moving cabins, plumbing, installing a power system from outboard motors, and an automatic washing machine. Needless to say, Orville was the only one who could start the engines which pumped the water or operated the railway from the dock.

For Orville, the Island with its mechanical problems and potential for "puttering" became his refuge during the Smithsonian controversy and the myriad of committees, dinners and award ceremonies which now cluttered his life. It was also a wonderful place for his nieces, nephews, and special friends to visit. At Kitty Hawk he had enjoyed hunting; at Lambert Island which he owned until 1941, he rediscovered the delights of fishing.

Orville was not the only one who appreciated Lambert Island. As a reporter for the *Kansas City Star* Katharine's Oberlin math tutor, Harry Haskell supported Orville in the Smithsonian dispute and was a frequent and welcome visitor when he was in the Dayton area.

SMITHSONIAN AND ROMANCE—1920's

While Orville was a major in charge of production and aviation consultation during World War I, two of his former pilot trainees distinguished themselves: Henry "Hap" Arnold who was later installed as Chief of Army Air Forces and Roy Brown, the Canadian who shot down the infamous German pilot, the Red Baron. The US government settled the patent problems with a three million dollar fee and a licensing agreement. The First Flyer, which had survived the Dayton Flood, found a home in London as the result of Charles Walcott's insistence that Langley's Aerodrome deserved Smithsonian honors, not the Wright plane. Most Americans felt the Wright Brothers had been wronged and insulted by the Museum's decision.

When Walcott died in the late 20's, he was replaced by Charles Abbott who immediately began to negotiate with Orville to return the plane to the United States. What Abbott didn't understand was that the Wrights did not negotiate or compromise. Orville wrote a detailed letter requesting the Smithsonian admit the modifications which Curtiss made on the Langley Aerodrome, remove the word CAPABLE from its plaque, correct the erroneous articles about the First Flyer and exhibit the First Flyer as the first manned-powered aircraft.

Abbott, another friend of Langley and Walcott, ignored the letter and suggested a committee be formed to mediate the problem.

REUCHLIN—1861 to 1920

The eldest of the four Wright Brothers was also the most independent and rebellious. Reuchlin graduated from a teacher's program in Iowa and taught school in Adair where Milton had purchased a farm during his time as Bishop of the Mississippi Region. He returned to Indiana with the family and attended Hartsville College with brother Lorin for a brief time.

Finding a position as bookkeeper in Dayton, he married the daughter of a missionary. Susan and Milton refused their financial support of the new in-laws and a long-time conflict began. Reuchlin headed West where he found employment again keeping books and working in a railroad office. He had four children, one of whom died early. Reuchlin himself suffered ill health and bought a farm near Kansas City, hoping his health would improve by outdoor work.

More or less teaching himself the intricacies of the land and animals, he called himself a "money saver not a money maker". He specialized in seed corn and Jersey cattle. His wife Lulu felt he lacked ambition.

His children flew with Uncle Orville at Huffman Field and did visit their grandfather, aunt and uncles when finances were possible. Reuchlin wrote the eulogy which was read at Wilbur's funeral, but did not feel he deserved to share in Wilbur's estate.

Orville enjoyed the company of the Kansas nieces and nephew, inviting them to Hawthorn Hill and Lambert Island for vacation and even driving across country to attend a wedding.

After years of uneven health, Reuchlin died in 1920 and is buried in Forest Hill Memorial Park in Kansas City, Missouri. Again he remained the rebellious independent.

KATHARINE and HARRY

When Katharine heard her friend Isabel Haskell had lost her battle with cancer, she sent her former math tutor a letter of condolence. A correspondence began between tutor and student which became more and more personal. Both Harry and Katharine served on the Oberlin Board of Trustees. Harry also supported Orville in the Smithsonian controversy.

Strangely enough, neither Katharine or Orville recognized Harry's romantic interest.

For her friends and neighbors, it was quite apparent.

LUCINDA WILLIAMS Hawthorn Hill neighbor

That Kansas City reporter is at the Wrights again. Katharine tells Bethany that he comes to see Orville, but I know better. Orville sits on the veranda with them until his back starts paining him. Then he goes inside. Haskell stays with Katharine. I know I saw the two of them holding hands, but my daughter Bethany laughed and told me I saw shadows. Bethany still admires Miss Katharine for living her own life with her own interests. Right now Katharine's without a cause to march about and spends her time getting Orville to all those award dinners and committee meetings.

There went Orville into the house. Mr. Haskell pushes his chair closer to Katharine and reaches for her hand. Those were not shadows. I know something is going on.

ELIZABETH NEWMAN to her Oberlin friend

I'm taking a moment to write you the big news. Kate and I had tea yesterday after the Oberlin Trustee's meeting and guess who dropped by our table? Harry Haskell! You remember him from the boarding house, don't you? We all thought the two of them would get together, but you know men.

Well, I'll give up my entire shoe collection if I'm wrong, but I saw that look in his eye. That's a man in love. Have you heard anything? I so hope I'm right. Kate deserves some happiness. I'm so happy for her. Funny thing, I don't think she realizes how he feels.

DOROTHY KENDALL's response to Elizabeth

I could dance for joy at Kate's news, and then I'd like to tell Orville Wright just what I think. How can I be happy and sad at the same time? Harry has asked Kate to marry him, but she's not sure how Orville will react.

I told her Orville and Harry are friends, that he would understand. She doesn't think so.

She does admit she's fond of Harry. You should have seen her blush when she told me about the two of them picking blueberries at Lambert Island this summer when Orville went fishing. Elizabeth, does that remind you of apple picking with Herbert when the two of you were courting?

I reminded Kate she was fifty years old, and Orville can surely take care of himself, and the Grumbaughs still work for them. My goodness, it's one thing to love your family, but there's no point in forgetting you also have a life. Am I sounding like one of Kate's suffragettes?

Right now, Katharine and Harry are debating which one of them will break the news to Orville. Well, I've already told my family I intend to go to that wedding. Goodness knows we've waited long enough.

RACHEL NESBITT, Dayton classmate

I just heard it from Sadie Hampton. She still helps Carrie Grumbaugh when all the Wright nieces, nephews and cousins get together. My old friend Kate is getting married, married to an Oberlin classmate Sadie said. But that's not what makes me mad. I'm so glad Orville never courted my sister Trudy. That man is spoiled worse than food left outside the icebox.

After all these years at Hawthorn Hill, Orville won't let Katharine have her wedding there. In fact, he hardly spoke to her when she and Mr. Haskell told him their intentions. She packed her belongings and made arrangements to be married at Oberlin. Orville did not attend the services.

I know Kate is heart broken. All the memories they shared, she has to be the one who is hurt. The Haskells have already moved to Kansas City. Sadie says Carrie promised to look after Orville and to keep in touch with Katharine. Sadie says brother Lorin tries to talk to him, but Orville just walks into another room.

They say Orville can't or won't accept the fact that Katharine would dare to leave him.

ELIZABETH to DOROTHY

It's not fair. Kate and Harry were planning a trip to Italy. You know how she always loved Latin and Roman history. Harry had just left Mayo Clinic when Kate came down with pneumonia which got worse and worse.

I can't believe she's dead. The newspaper says she will be buried in Dayton. Do you know anything about that?

DOROTHY to ELIZABETH

I've only heard that her brother Lorin convinced Orville to go see her. They say he arrived the day before she died, and she recognized him. Harry and Orville agreed that Katharine should be buried in the family plot in Woodland in Dayton.

What a shame they all couldn't have agreed that easily about the wedding! But I'm thankful that Kate and Harry had their tine together.

RACHEL NESBITT

Well, I was glad to see Orville and Katharine's husband walking together after the hearse on its way to Woodland Cemetery. I just hope Orville feels ashamed over the way he treated them. I hear Mr. Haskell is donating a fountain in her honor at Oberlin.

About time someone appreciated Katharine spent helping her father and brothers, giving up her teaching job to help Orville after that crash, traveling with them. Yes, she met a lot of important people, but I'm glad she finally had the opportunity to share a few years with a husband. I'm just so sad she didn't have more time with him.

I was about ready to leave the cemetery when I heard the planes flying overhead in military formation. At the grave they dipped in salute. Orville must have arranged that. About time he did something right!

But the anger dissolved when I saw what dropped from the planes. Roses! Enough to nearly blanket her grave. I couldn't move. I couldn't see through the tears.

It was a beautiful tribute, and Katharine deserved every petal. She encouraged and supported both those brothers, especially Orville.

God bless her.

KATHARINE WRIGHT HASKELL 1874-1929

Katharine was the only living daughter of the family and the youngest child. Born three years later on Orville's birthday, the two were especially close. When her mother died, Katharine inherited the household duties at the age of 15 with the help of a hired girl, Carrie Kayler Grumbach, who spent her life caring for the Bishop and his three younger children. Like their father, Orville and Katharine entertained Lori's children, attended poetry readings, concerts and other events.

Katharine helped Wilbur nurse Orville's serious bout with typhoid fever. Upon her return to Oberlin College, she ended her engagement to a football player. Katharine was one of the first to believe and support Wilbur's dream of flying. After Orville's

Fort Meyer's crash, she stayed with him and accompanied him to Europe instead of teaching Latin at Dayton Steele High School. With her conversational skills, cheerful attitude, and ability to remember names and faces, she was a definite asset as their social secretary in Europe and the United States.

Back in Dayton she accompanied Orville on many of his public appearances after Wilbur's death and organized family visits at both Hawthorn Hill and Lambert Island, became an Oberlin Trustee, and corresponded with classmates. Mabel Beck, Wilbur's secretary, now arranged Orville's meetings.

A letter of condolence to her former math tutor Harry Haskell of the *Kansas City Star* developed into romance. Katharine suspected Orville would not approve, and she was correct.

When he was told, he stopped speaking to her, believing she had forsaken him. Harry and Katharine were married at Oberlin in 1926 and moved to Kansas City without contact from Orville. The Haskells planned a trip to Italy, but Katharine fell ill with pneumonia.Orville arrived at Kansas City the day before she died in 1929.

She was buried in Dayton's Woodland cemetery in the family plot after nearly three years of marriage.

CHARLES LINDBERG

A month after the successful flight of *The Spirit of St. Louis* in 1927, Charles Lindbergh landed on a Dayton runway where Orville Wright was waiting to meet him. Their admiration was quick and mutual. While the Wrights had waited years for Dayton's recognition, the citizens of Dayton lined the streets to catch a glimpse of their new hero of flight. Beside him, Orville smiled proudly on their way for a private time at Hawthorn Hill. The people of Dayton had other ideas and hurried to the spacious Hawthorn Hill lawn. They cheered and crowded closer and closer to the door.

To calm them, Orville convinced Lindbergh to wave from the upstairs balcony. The plan was successful, and the two aviators were able to enjoy a private, peaceful lunch.

Meeting Orville became an important event for all important people who came to Dayton, but Lindbergh's reception was by far the most special. In 1940 when Franklin Roosevelt arrived, Orville insisted on leaving the President's car at the foot of the drive and walking alone to the house. No private luncheon. No waving from the balcony. As far as Orville was concerned aviation was more important than politics.

1930'S

Veteran's Administration formed, Franklin Delano Roosevelt elected, US banks closed, Philippines given independence. Congress lends 1 ½ billion to help economy, US Federal Reserve reorganized, minimum wage for women, Unemployment insurance law enacted. Ex-servicemen march on Washington to demand their bonuses—2000 are driven out by McArthur, Work begins on Golden Gate Bridge, Empire State Building opens, Prohibition repealed, January becomes Inauguration Day, Social Security Act, Dillinger shot, Al Capone jailed for tax evasion, Lindberg baby kidnapped. John L. Lewis calls United Mineworkers strike to show power, Roosevelt appeals Italy and Germany for peace, ambassadors recalled. US economy improves with European purchases of arms and military equipment.

Hitler becomes German dictator, erects concentration camps, boycott of Jews begins, invades Poland. France begins to build Maginot Line Spanish Civil War, first bombing of a city (Guernica), Hitler and Mussolini form alliance, Franco replaces Spanish king. Japanese begin seizing Chinese cities.

George VI crowed king, replacing his brother, Churchill warns of German air reserves, Amy Johnson flies solo from London to Australia. Amelia Earhart lost in flight across Pacific First US aircraft carrier launched.

LITERATURE/FILMS

Maxwell Anderson, John Hersey, Dashiell Hammett, Katherine Anne Porter, Pearl S. Buck, Wm. Saroyan, Richard Wright, Archibald McLeish, James Hilton—Blondie comic strip—Orson Wells panics radio listeners to his broadcast of *War of the Worlds*

FILMS *Gone With the Wind, Wizard of Oz, Stagecoach, Mutiny on the Bounty*—Marlene Dietrich, Greta Garbo, Clark Gable, Shirley Temple

ART/MUSIC

Grandma Moses, Cole Porter, Rogers and Hart, *Star Spangled Banner* chosen as National Anthem. Hammond organ popular, Harvard presents honorary degree to Marian Anderson. Popular songs: *Easter Parade, Night and Day, Good Night, Sweetheart, I Got Rhythm, Stardust, Blue Moon, Whistle While You Work, Harbor Lights, The Last Time I Saw Paris, Over the Rainbow, God Bless America*

SCIENCE, SPORTS, ETC

Balloons and radar warn Britain of German aerial attacks. Women and children evacuated from London. Planet Pluto discovered. Balloon tires for farm tractors, Flash bulbs. Contract bridge. Alcoholics Anonymous. Baseball Hall of Fame. Howard Hughes flies around the world. First All-Star Baseball game, Turbo jet engine developed. Nylon patented, first nylon stockings. Baseball first televised in US, Pan Am flies commercial from NY to Europe.

HONORS AND MONUMENTS

A high school dropout, Orville was awarded nearly a dozen honorary degrees including those from Yale and Harvard. In the interim Orville and Wilbur were honored by several memorials. The first one, a small one in Kitty Hawk, had been arranged by their old friend Bill Tate. The second was near Pau, France, where Wilbur first flew in Europe. This one was damaged by the Germans in World War II.

A number of people feel Huffman Field is the most important of the major American monuments. Torrence Huffman donated the field which was the proving ground for the first practical aircraft. This land later became part of the Wright—Patterson Air Force Base.

The largest and best known memorial is on Kill Devil Hill, instigated by a North Carolina congressman to increase tourism to his state. A highway replaced the privately owned boats which had originally brought the Brothers to Nags Head and the large monument in their honor became the center of tourist attractions. The major problem in building the imposing monument was the dune movement. They found a way to anchor the dune, and in 1932 Orville and Amelia Earhart dedicated the cornerstone. This memorial has attracted tourists and aviation enthusiasts from all over the world. For many of them, this is the only part of the Wright story they ever learn.

In 1950, Carillon Park was opened in Dayton, thanks to the effort of Orville's friend Edward Deeds, the new CEO of the National Cash Register Company. This Park has a building dedicated to the Wrights and joins Wright Patterson and Huffman Field as the Birthplace of Aviation. This contains a more complete picture of the Brothers and the construction of the First Flyer. The State of Ohio considers itself the Birthplace of Aviation and proudly proclaims the fact on its license plates. Orville arranged for personal letters, several copies of the ledgers Milton used as his Diary and Orville's bicycle race medals in the library at Wright State University.

Lindbergh suggested Orville write an autobiography of their lives and path to success, but Orville still preferred puttering to writing. Earl Findley and John McMahon were not so hesitant and were quickly reprimanded for inaccurate or exaggerated reporting about their private lives and the development of the plane. Again Orville insisted on correct information and appreciation for the ingenuity and logic of Brother Wilbur. Findley and McMahon were immediately dismissed as biographers. Orville didn't want to share their private lives, nor did he want to interpret the thoughts and goals of his brothers. For Orville, the importance was in what they had done, not the why. He also insisted on reading manuscripts for technical errors.

Under a great deal of government pressure, a committee headed by Charles Lindbergh, began searching for a way to bring the First Flyer back to the United States. Lindbergh suggested concentrating on the modifications Curtiss had made in an effort to fly the Aerodrome. After Lindbergh's personal tragedy, he resigned from the committee. Abbott suggested replacement by a political group. Orville refused. He felt certain the new group would ignore his observations. He, therefore, accepted Henry Ford's offer to secure their first Dayton home and bicycle shop in his special exhibit. For Orville, this was another monument to their achievements.

GREENFIELD VILLAGE

While most Americans had sided with Orville's decision to move the First Flyer to England, the inhabitants of Dayton rebelled at the rumor of moving the Wright home and a bicycle shop to Henry Ford's exhibit of famous places near Detroit. Ford already had Edison's museum, Luther Burbank's plant laboratory and Stephen Foster's home to name a few. Again it was Orville's determination to perpetuate their accomplishment that he considered the offer. Katharine had sold their childhood home, and Orville feared that others might shatter the simplicity of their lives on Hawthorn Street. While Daytonians might disapprove, Orville agreed with Ford. The house was carefully removed and rebuilt on the Ford property where it remains next to the Bicycle Shop. Ford hired Wright mechanic Charles Taylor to help authenticate the bicycle shop.

Orville dedicated the Wright Exhibit on Wilbur's birthday, April 16, 1938.

JACOB HORNER insisted on one last ride down Hawthorn Street to say good bye to the house and shop he had always associated with the Brothers.

I had to come by. Wish I could get out of the car and take a last walk down the street, but I'm stuck in this wheel chair. My boy Andrew just shakes his head. But he doesn't understand. This was the place where dreams began to shape, to find their foundations. It would be a comfort to walk down to the bicycle shop and remember those two Brothers scrapping and then to look to the sky when I hear the motor of an airplane.

They went so much further than we expected. Most of us laughed at them, but they taught us to believe in the impossible. I never picked up a bolt in that bicycle shop, but I found out that it's important to work hard and try again if you fail. I never was at that Hawthorn Hill place, never met any of their important friends. It wouldn't have been right to pretend I'd been a part of their success.

I am proud of them for not giving in to our laughter at their hard work. That kind of pride strengthens a man. They touched us all and made us more tolerant of new ideas, of the impossible.

Take me home, Andrew. I want to remember it the way it was. To wonder when Ed Sines is going to open the print shop, to hear the Brothers' scrapping, to smell Charlie Taylor's cigars when I passed the bicycle shop, hear Orville's mandolin in the evening, or sniff one of Carrie's pot roast stews.

I lived during a good time.

SADIE HAMPTON

Why do I always forget my hankie? Mind you now, I didn't even consider the thought I might cry. Should have known better.

You won't believe this, but I even cried when they laid Katharine to rest. That's something I never expected I'd do. She would have loved seeing them drop those roses. Well, maybe she did, who knows?

That Henry Ford ordered his men to take down the house, and I reckon they're gonna rebuild it up in Michigan. Makes me mad to think about it! The Wrights lived and worked here, not in Detroit. They took down the kitchen last week. I don't think I could have watched that, remembering Wilbur coming in from work and eating a cracker while he waited for his evening meal. And all them recipes Katharine brought for us to fix for her guests. The extra washing for them foreigners and trying to keep all that silver polished. Yes, I got a lot of memories about this house, and I sure to goodness wish they'd keep it here.

The newspapers said Orville wanted to preserve the house. He may be right about people forgetting it here and letting it get remodeled or run down. I wouldn't like that neither. I guess I'll just have to keep it here in my memories.

Visitors continued to pay homage to the first man to fly, and Orville served on many committees and received additional awards. Those honors were not enough. Orville wanted the First Flyer placed with honors in the Smithsonian. Lindbergh and writer Fred Kelly tried to solve the problem and bring the Flyer home. The government pressured Charles Abbott to solve the problem.

Thanks to Fred Kelly's quiet negotiations, Orville's carefully prepared list of modifications about the Aerodrome was published as a separate document and to repudiate the incomplete information of other writers. The truth was finally accepted. Orville wrote a letter changing his Will to allow the Flyer to come home. The letter went into his files. He also contacted the English museum where the Flyer had been moved to protect it from foreign bombers. Now, all he had to do was wait for the impending war to end. With all the military concerns, Orville didn't announce his decision to the Smithsonian. Fred Kelly earned Orville's appreciation and began to write the only authorized biography of the Brothers and their achievement. As usual Orville insisted on checking the manuscript for technical and personal errors.

LORIN WRIGHT—1862 to 1939

The second son of the Wrights was the advisor. A bookkeeper by profession he lived in Dayton with his wife and four children. For a brief time, he stayed in Doge City where he collected stories of the West and delighted his family and friends by sharing them. He and Reuchlin delighted teasing Wilbur when they were boys.

After his mother's death, Lorin was the one who eased Katharine's teenage grief by suggesting she press flowers in memory of Susan's love for them. Katharine's book of pressed flowers stayed with her for years. He handled the banking for the Brothers and helped manage the aviation company since Orville didn't enjoy meetings. After the company closed, he encouraged Orville to design and sell Flips and Flops which were similar to family toy they had enjoyed. When those sales declined, Orville designed small, advertising gliders and a small printing press to make them. Lorin's children and spouses continued visiting and debating with Uncle Orv.

When Orville refused to forgive Katharine for leaving him, it was Lorin who insisted that Orville go to Kansas City when she was ill. Both of them were there when she died.

Lorin was also buried in Woodland Cemetery, but with his own family rather than with parents and siblings.

1940's

WORLD WAR II

Germany invades Norway and Denmark, London blitz, Dunkirk evacuates stranded troops, submarine attacks intensify, Japan, Germany and Italy sign pact, Belgium surrenders, North African offensive: El Alamain, Rommel plans European defense, Germany invades Russia, Japan attack Pearl Harbor, Bataan forced prisoner march, Doolittle bombs Tokyo. McArthur—chief of Far East Forces, Eisenhower—chief of North Africa then European defense, Polish massacre by Germans, Germans use U-2 rockets, FDR wins third term, Churchill—Prime minister, US regains Pacific Islands, Aleutians, and invades Italy, Britain invades Burma. Mussolini killed by Partisans, Battle of Bulge, Hitler commits suicide, Yalta Conference, FDR dies, Harry S. Truman president, United Nations Charter signed, V-E Day ends European War, Atom bombs used on Japan, V-J Day, Three-power occupation of Berlin, Nuremburg Trials begin.

POST WAR POLITICS

Viet Nam declares independence from France, Juan Peron—president of Argentina, DeGaulle—Provisional French president, UN plans Arab-Jew partition of Israel, Gandhi demands independence from Britain, is assassinated, Nehru becomes Indian Premier, Berlin Blockade begins. Truman wins over Dewey, Chiang Kai Shek moves his government to Formosa, Apartheid in South Africa.

LITERATURE/FILMS

Lloyd Douglas, James Thurber, Ray Bradbury, Gwendolyn Brooks, Carson McCullers, Margaret Mead, Benjamin Spock, Ernie Pyle, James A. Michener, Mickey Spillane. Norman Mailer, Kinsey researches and writes *Sexual Behavior of Human Male.*
Radio: Jack Benny, FibberMcGee and Molly, The Lone Ranger, The Shadow
Going My Way-Bing Crosby, Dead Sea Scrolls found.

MUSIC/ART

Jackson Pollack, Diego Rivera murals. **Songs:** *When You Wish Upon a Star, Deep in the Heart, of Texas, Chattanooga Choo Choo, Oh! What a Beautiful Morning, Don't Fence Me In, Rudolph, the Red Nosed Reindeer, Some Enchanted Evening, Sentimental Journey, Shoo Fly Pie and Apple Pan Dowdy.*
Rogers and Hammerstein—*South Pacific.* Bartok, Leonard Bernstein, Balanchine Ballet forms, Maria Callas debuts, Duke Ellington popular composer and jazz pianist, samba introduced.

SCIENCE

Rh blood factor, First helicopter flight, new combustion for jet engines, First tests of jet planes, portable military bridges, Manhattan Project for atomic bomb, Dacron invented, Oil line opens from Texas to Pennsylvania, Airplanes at supersonic speeds, Transistor invented, USSR tests its A-Bomb, Air Force jet crosses US in 3 hours, 46 minutes

SPORTS, ETC

Jack Dempsey and Joe Louis retire from boxing, Supreme Court restricts working hours for 16-18 year olds, Sugar, coffee, gas, shoes, meat, cheese and canned foods rationed during War, OPA freezes wages, salaries and prices to curb inflation, Government takes over coal mines during a strike, European Black market for food, clothing and cigarettes. Empire State Building struck by B-25 (US) bomber, Over 100 million vets enroll in college with G. I. Bill of Rights, Jackie Robinson is first major league black baseball player.

THE LAST DAYS

While the personal Wright information went to Wright State, Orville sent the technical information to the Library of Congress which was now directed by Archibald McLeish and his assistant James McFarland. Neither of these men had been part of the previous political group who had insisted Langely's efforts surpassed that of the Wright Brothers.

In November 1947, Orville suffered a heart attack while running up the steps of the National Cash Register building. He was told to slow down and take it easy.

Brenda Meyers was a day shift nurse at the Dayton Hospital where Orville recuperated.

You'll never guess who was on my floor this last week. Yes, I know I shouldn't be talking about patients, but I've never met anyone so famous before. Orville Wright! Would you believe it? He was so polite, even teased me a little about counting out too many pills.

His cook and housekeeper laughed at that one. "We all know he's feeling better, but he sure did give us a scare—a man his age running up stairs. I wouldn't be surprised if he asked for a bicycle to ride home."

I shook my head in disbelief—a man who invented an airplane and speeded through Dayton in his car? A bike would be much too slow for him!

"You know he used to win medals back when everyone raced bikes."

Still not believing her, I just nodded and changed the subject. "You know he was asking us for some tools last night."

The cook was still laughing when one of the nephews came in to see him.

"You know he must be feeling better, Carrie." He hugged her. "That's the best news I've had." He turned to me. "When Uncle Orv begins taking things apart or fixing them, we know he's on the mend."

I looked around.

Mr. Wright's voice sounded a bit weak, but his eyes twinkled with mischief. "I thought of a way to improve these oxygen tents. Just wanted to do a bit of tinkering before I went home."

He grinned in Carrie's direction. "You still going to ride over here to take me home."

"Better save your strength to answer your mail." She handed him two envelopes.

I could see one was from the White House and shivered at the thought. You just never know what people are like. One day he's teasing me about the pills, and the next he's reading a letter from the President. He's had quite a life, this Orville Wright. Just think about it. I've heard he used to fly kites in the sky, and now he watches jet planes. I wonder if he'd like to fly one?

In January, Orville had just fixed a door knob when the second heart attack hit. This one was fatal. Orville would not be dedicating the First Flyer. But, he did make a few more headlines. The Wrights had expected Mabel Beck to be named executor of this estate. Instead he chose two of his nephews in law. The Smithsonian waited for instructions. Orville had never presented the letter granting permission to acknowledge and display the First Flyer. Mabel Beck denied the letter's existence. After being reminded of her duty to fulfill Orville's wishes, she produced the letter.

The Flyer was coming home.

The third problem was more personal. Where to have the funeral service? Although Orville was not a member, the family chose The First Baptist Church which was large enough for family and friends.

Orville was put to rest in the family plot with his parents, Katharine and Wilbur. A military formation of jets dipped in salute.

Nieces and nephews attended the placement of the Flyer at the Smithsonian and the dedication of Carillon Park in Dayton. Fred Kelly's two books about the Brothers remained in print for over fifty years. Orville had protected the Wright legacy.

What made them so successful?

Milton and Susan Wright encouraged curiosity, logic and a work ethic. From their brother Reuchlin, they observed honor and individualism, from Lorin, sensitivity for the feelings of others and a good sense of business. Katharine encouraged and supported them when many others thought the Brothers wasted their time. Wilbur had a dream and, unlike many dreamers, had the perseverance to build its foundations. Orville could always be counted on to provide the unusual solutions.

Together they established a family legacy which led to one of mankind's great achievements.

WILBUR WRIGHT BIRTHPLACE PRESERVATION SOCIETY

Kitty Hawk—First Flight

Dayton—First aircraft

Millville—FIRST STEPS

Site purchased by State of Indiana—1920's

Promoted by local citizens—1920's to 1990's

Birth Home vandalized and razed—1950's

Home rebuilt—1970's

Low attendance threatens closure—1980's

Deeded to volunteer, non-profit group—1995

THE BIRTHPLACE PRESERVATION SOCIETY

Dedicated to sharing the story of the Wrights Brothers and their family as they followed a dream and unlocked the secrets of manned-powered flight.

www.wwbirthplace.org; wilbur@nltc.net; 765-332-2495

LOCATION: East Central Indiana I-70 Wilbur Wright exit between Richmond and New Castle. Turn north.

SR 38—turn north on Wilbur Wright Road between Hagerstown and New Castle.

SR 36 turn south on Wilbur Wright Road between Mt. Summit and Losantsville.

In all cases, follow the brown airplane signs after leaving a state or national road.

Site: Birth Home and farm buildings

Museum:

Full-sized replica First Flyer model

Kitty Hawk camp

1903 Main Street

Photos, sketches, and memorabilia displays

Festivals: The Birthplace Festival in June

Christmas Tree Walk in November

Share the story of the Wright Family with us and visitors from around the world.

BIBLIOGRAPHY

THE BISHOP'S BOYS by Tom Crouch

THE WRIGHT BROTHERS by Frank Kelly

MIRACLE AT KITTY HAWK by Frank Kelly

THE WRIGHT SISTER by Richard Maurer

TRIUMPH AT KITTY HAWK by Thomas C. Parramore

TO CONQUER THE AIR by James Tobin

FIRST FLIGHT by T. A. Heppenheimer

THE FLYERS by Noah Adams

ON GREAT WHITE WINGS by Gulick and Dunmore

WILBUR AND ORVILLE by Fred Howard

TIMETABLES of HISTORY (Third Revised Edition) by Grun

FROM BICYCLE TO BIPLANE by John Fisk

WRIGHT REMINISCENCES by niece Ivonette Wright Miller

DIARY of MILTON WRIGHT

Letters and photos from WRIGHT STATE UNIVERSITY, Dayton, HUNTINGTON COLLEGE, Huntington, IN, Indianapolis Motor Speedway concerning the Wright's Exhibition there in 1910.